Allen & Unwin's House of Books aims to bring Australia's cultural and literary heritage to a broad audience by creating affordable print and ebook editions of the nation's most significant and enduring writers and their work. The fiction, non-fiction, plays and poetry of generations of Australian writers that were published before the advent of ebooks will now be available to new readers, alongside a selection of more recently published books that had fallen out of circulation.

The House of Books is an eloquent collection of Australia's finest literary achievements.

Kylie Tennant was the author of nine novels, plus short stories, plays, journalism, criticism and biography as well as much writing for children. She is noted for her social realist studies of urban and rural working-class life from the 1930s, that began with *Tiburon* (1935), and included *Foveaux* (1939), named after a street in the slums of Surry Hills.

Her working life encompassed such jobs as a barmaid, reviewer, church sister and publicist for the ABC. Seeking to be true to the society she observed, she took to the road with itinerant workers in the worst years of the Depression, and went so far as to spend a week in gaol for the sake of research.

Tennant was born in Manly, New South Wales, in 1912 and died in 1988. She was awarded the Order of Australia in 1980.

KYLIE TENNANT

The Man on the Headland

This edition published by Allen & Unwin House of Books in 2012
First published by Angus & Robertson Publishers Pty Ltd, Sydney, in 1971

Copyright © Kylie Tennant 1971

All rights reserved. No part of this book may be reproduced or transmitted in any form or by any means, electronic or mechanical, including photocopying, recording or by any information storage and retrieval system, without prior permission in writing from the publisher. The Australian *Copyright Act 1968* (the Act) allows a maximum of one chapter or 10 per cent of this book, whichever is the greater, to be photocopied by any educational institution for its educational purposes provided that the educational institution (or body that administers it) has given a remuneration notice to Copyright Agency Limited (CAL) under the Act.

Allen & Unwin
Sydney, Melbourne, Auckland, London

83 Alexander Street
Crows Nest NSW 2065
Australia
Phone: (61 2) 8425 0100
Fax: (61 2) 9906 2218
Email: info@allenandunwin.com
Web: www.allenandunwin.com

Cataloguing-in-Publication details are available
from the National Library of Australia
www.trove.nla.gov.au

ISBN 978 1 74331 362 6 (pbk)
ISBN 978 1 74343 077 4 (ebook)

Printed and bound in Australia by Griffin Press

The paper in this book is FSC® certified. FSC® promotes environmentally responsible, socially beneficial and economically viable management of the world's forests.

Chapter I

LEAGUE AFTER LEAGUE the headlands curve up the coast of the continent. The white fingers of the sea play on them, each bluff giving out its unique note, making its own music. When the waves surge in under the golden arch of basalt at Diamond Head, between the ledges dripping with weed and cunjevoi, you can hear the boom from the cliff-top with the surge of the bombora and the boom again. This roar comes not only from the golden arch but all around a half-mile of rocks and cliff; squeaks of tiny beaches of red and green pebbles rolling, slate-coloured and cream and mauve pebbles straining in the froth, quiet pools of shells and limpets, the undertow from fishermen's platform rocks and tumbled stone.

The song goes up the cliffs with the quivering heat of grey driftwood, the scent of seaweed and dry grass, up where the track winds higher than the sea-hawk hovering to the ridge-top where the spray gives way to flannel flowers and golden everlastings, pale violets, thick wrinkled banksias holding out honeycombs for the gill-birds. All the froth of flowers splashes over the great dragon-spine slanting inland, rearing up above the sea its crown of glittering quartz.

Diamond Head has its own special illusion. Anyone who comes there is seized with a wild resolution to stay for ever. No man but is possessed with the urge to bend Diamond Head to his secret longings, to make it his own. Diamond Head deals with them. It outlasts. Its great bulk of basalt was doing just this a few hundred years ago when Captain Cook and his crew of constipated heroes swept past, claiming the continent in a distant and gentlemanly manner. They heard the roar of the cliffs as so many cheers for their passing, a bombardment of welcome salutes. And Diamond Head will give a belch and a roar for the passing of all who come after him.

When Cook sailed past it was a grey May day as cold as the captain's eye. There would be a steely light on the sea, the sails stretched by the following southerly wind. Coming round Crowdy Head they would have kept well out to avoid the tail of foam on the Mermaid Reef. So that Cook must have been looking through the spyglass to see the black stick figures of aborigines on our headland and log it as Indian Head.

"Of the aborigines and their manner of life," he wrote elsewhere, "we know little as we have never been able to form the least connection with them."

In my mind's eye there is blown smoke from the crest where the aborigines are. They are sending a message inland of the unknown flying object on the sea, concentrating the picture of it. The smoke is only a signal that they are about to send. The message would go to the three peaks across the lake which Cook named the Three Brothers, on to the Comboyne Range and to the Great Dividing Range, the high plateau where, being human, the relay men would begin to get it wrong. Cook by this time would be 'way up the coast, headlands dropping behind, with a thousand and three hundred miles before him.

The real reason for the aborigines being on the crown of Diamond Head would be that they were digging for quartz crystals to tip their tools, grubbing low-grade industrial diamonds out of the clay pockets. They dug powock, an edible root, on the swampy plains behind Diamond Head and fished the long beaches, found pipis in the sand and used the river crossing seven miles north at Point Perpendicular which they later showed the white explorers. But by the time the Metcalfes came to Diamond Head the aborigines were gone, all gone, like the smoke blown from their fires.

In 1770 when the great captain swept past our headland Ernie Metcalfe's great-grandfather was a poacher on the Welsh mountains. I see the aborigines running like shadows and a line of Metcalfes running like deer before the men who hunt down men. Ernie's grandfather was transported for taking a pheasant for a bet and I always see him as a young man. He has inherited his grandson's sardonic manner, his arched nose and hazel eyes, the curls touched with bronze as Ernie's were when we first knew him. Indeed I am not sure that it is not Ernie who is stepping off the ship and looking about him, light-footed and alert. He has the expression he had when he went off to fight World War I for the country that sentenced his grandfather.

But World War II had come on before we met Ernie. If we understood time—and nobody does—we should probably find patterns in it, but it is simpler to call it chance that directed our three lives so that Ernie and the two Rodds were converging on a fly-speck fishing village on the North Coast of New South Wales. And if you think that it was hard on the little town of Laurieton that three such queer characters were arriving at the one time, remember that then the town seven miles north of Diamond Head at what was once an aboriginal river crossing had not yet grown its paunch of prosperity, was already charged with queer characters and well able to take care of itself.

Chapter II

Ernie travelled slowest and was the first to arrive. He came down the coast from Queensland in the old sulky, taking it easy not to tire the horse or the dogs padding behind. The blue cattle bitch that Ernie called Ole Mammy had a little pup and part of the time she travelled with it on the tarpaulin that covered all Ernie's worldly goods, his miner's tools, his other suit, a ground sheet and blankets, the camp oven, the "bit of tucker". The water-bag swung below the sulky covered in dust.

Ernie was just coming home to Diamond Head on a visit to see "the sister" and his brother Jack. He had liked Queensland and had spent years roaming and foraging over it from the Gulf to the tablelands. Originally he had travelled up to see his brother Charlie, who had a sheep property out from Winton, but no two Metcalfes could be together without one of them telling the other how to run the farm. After Ernie had advised Charlie on the proper rearing of sheep there was one final argument and Ernie left to do a bit of gold fossicking. In the Depression he lived on the dole. He was an expert fencer, he could handle a pick and shovel. "The navvy," Ernie always said, "is the gentleman of the working class."

Neatly tucked away under his well-shaped skull were all he needed—skills, memories, nuggets of pure intelligence, jokes, a few useless foibles, and seventy thousand different varieties of observation on everything under the sun. For although Ernie was close-mouthed about himself and his own affairs he was one of the world's great talkers. He was solitary but sociable and he made friends easily. Like most bushmen he could make anything he wanted with his own hands.

Under his slouched old army hat his eyes were as green as a sunlit clearing and his expression was that of the Laughing Cavalier who on suburban walls reminds the wistful dwellers of what they have lost. But the Cavalier is fat and Ernie would never be fat. He was too energetic. As he came slowly down the coast, the reins loose, he rolled cigarettes as a man fingers praying beads. The blue sea, dodging behind trees and the turns of the road, kept him company. And there rode with Ernie also, a companion of a sort, an acquaintance to whom he paid little attention—Death.

Ernie treated Death as he would a drunk trying to borrow money. He was good-humoured but ready to give him the slip, more occupied with the prospects of a camp for the night, with water and a pick for the horse.

When the sulky at last came slowly down the broad main thoroughfare of Laurieton where cows roamed the wayside grass under the camphor-laurel trees, the blue estuary was just as it had always been, sea-banks uncovered at low tide, mangroves clicking with crabs, fishing birds stalking, the breakwater of great rocks holding off the surf where the Camden Haven River met the sea below the coastguards' cottages and the lighthouse. The river bank smelt of dried seaweed, tar, decayed fish-heads and mud. Over Laurieton in the late afternoon fell the shadow of the Big Brother like the pointer of a sundial advancing down towards the sea as the sun sank behind the mountain.

Ernie had decided to spend the night with his niece Dot, who had married Athol Stace, the owner of a snapper boat. The Staces had once owned a timber mill, but the big timber was almost cut out around the Camden Haven, and Longworths had the mill with its sawdust pile smoking blue in a curve of the river. Ernie would catch up on the news, play with Dot's children, give the horse a rest, and maybe stroll down to the hotel for a beer. In the morning, as soon as Sam the puntman was ready to take him across, Ernie would cover the last seven miles south to Diamond Head.

Sam was a morose character, slowly turning the puntwheel by hand, shining drops and strands of weeds circling and falling back like unheard prayers. But Sam was old enough to recognize Ernie as one of the Metcalfes of Diamond Head, the roving one who never settled down.

It took us longer to make our way there. We had been planning for years and were not like Ernie, who merely slung the camp gear on the sulky. We were the Rodds and when we married bets were taken that it wouldn't last a year, but at the end of ten years we were still the Rodds, who would leave off arguing with each other to unite in arguing with anyone else. We were born seven years apart under the sign of the Poor Fish who are tied together by their tails and trying to go in opposite directions. Frequently and dramatically we offered each other a divorce, an offer instantly accepted and never acted on.

When we decided to go in the same direction nothing could stop us, but we first had to disentangle ourselves from all the other claims, plans, obstructions and entanglements.

We had made up our minds instantly to go to Laurieton when we called to see a friend. We had never heard of the place before. One holiday we called to visit J.N. who was a school inspector and an enthusiast. He had caught enthusiasm young and was a regular Typhoid Mary, infecting anyone susceptible to ideas and optimism. He loved humanity and wanted to write, but while he could tell a good story, as soon as he put it on paper he killed it stone dead. Our mission was to break the news that some poor little tale he had sent was irretrievably mangled and after asking if none of the three endings he had suggested could possibly revive it he changed the subject.

"Now there's where you should go to write a book. The place is in my inspectorate on the North Coast and the old chap there wants to come to Sydney. It's on the edge of the river just a mile from the sea. Surfing beaches," J.N. carolled, "the school has its own oyster lease."

A gleam came up behind Roddy's glasses. He loved oysters but he loved surfing more.

"You could teach, Roddy, and Kylie could write. Fishermen and cattle-stealers! Miles of lonely bush, lakes, mountains..."

"The children are little savages," his wife put in. "The town girls have a Ladies' Football Team. The men burn each other's nets and steal anything that isn't nailed down."

"Peaceful, beautiful, unspoilt," J.N. continued. "Now what you must do, Roddy, is put in to Head Office before it falls vacant. Get your application in right away."

Head Office treated the application with *hauteur*. A pretty thing if every teacher whose wife was a writer wanted to get himself shifted about to suit her! Was the whole List to be altered for a wife's whim? Never! They offered Rodd other and larger schools, which he declined. His conduct, lacking in ambition, was something Head Office could not countenance or approve.

At that time Rodd was deputy head of a high school in a town in the Hunter River Valley. When we arrived the town reservoir showed an interesting pattern of cracked earth, and if you turned on a tap nothing but black mud fell out. The water in the house tanks had to be saved for drinking. The river was a drain choked with rusty tins, old motor tyres and rubbish.

The town had the usual furnishings of churches, butter factory, a coal-mine, banks, shops and social ambitions. The temperature sometimes rose to 103 degrees and stayed above the hundred mark for days. Some nights we slept in the back yard until the iron roof of our house cooled down and we were once nearly trodden on by a horse which had learnt to lift the gate-latch.

Our house was not in the town, which had slipped down into a gullet between the hills, but up on a plateau where in better times clouds and mirages swept over miles of open paddock. The sheep could be seen frantically running, following a truck laden with boughs cut to provide them with a little food.

I swore there were ghosts. Roddy said it was the horse who could lift the gate-latch. I insisted that sometimes at night a dark, malevolent wave came across the paddocks from the direction of a distant mountain peak. Even when the inhabitants of the town told him that over there had been the coal-mine of St Heliers where in the early days convicts worked in conditions of great cruelty he refused to believe me.

We had glorious roses and the soil would grow anything. Roddy was once, in a drought, prosecuted for watering the roses. At the same time one of his schoolgirls came up for sentence for selling wine to a passing troop train. Ever afterwards, Roddy claimed, she looked slightly patronizing but gave him an encouraging smile, recognizing a fellow law-breaker but one without much talent.

I used to cry as I typed with the sweat dripping on the typewriter and the iron roof heating up overhead. The cemetery near by was full of black, polished tombstones over the best people and I had formed an aversion for being buried there. Half-way through the year, still crying quietly, I was moved into hospital and the nurse said my inside was "just like a bargain sale" as they kept finding new pieces they could snatch with little cries of pleasure. From the upstairs room of the hospital I could see Roddy on the opposite hillslope in the school playground. The headmaster, a genial man, was himself dying of two conflicting ailments so he left to Roddy much of the running of the huge school. The headmaster, trained to "get on", accepted a new and even bigger school and didn't last the first term. So many headmasters, Head Office remarked, either had nervous breakdowns or perished inexplicably. The breed was not what it was once.

I was judging a short-story competition. The stories came in a packing case from the city and as I read each one I would sort it into another big box on the other side of the bed. They seemed mostly to be about people dying in hospital.

But you must not think we did not enjoy ourselves. We had hosts of friends and visitors, festivals, gifts and meetings. The ghosts did not really bother us. They were a change from the city slum in which I had written an earlier book. We had a house in an alley which travelled visitors said was just like Limehouse. It had fog when there was no fog anywhere else and our poor neighbours, to whom I used to chat, sitting on the front doorstep which was right on the footpath, often had drunken quarrels by night so that there would be blood on the pavement. You could have a hot bath by heating the copper in the back yard and there was one room and a kitchen downstairs and a room upstairs. We never used the upstairs room because it was crowded in every crack with bugs. A man used to come round on Saturday morning selling bug poison. At first we thought we would spray them. But a female bug, seeing death approaching, gathered her little ones behind her and faced us with defiant feelers. Imagine that! A female bug protecting her young! After this display of maternal courage we left them alone. The bugs, being slow thinkers, waited. They sent out scouts downstairs but they never came back. All in all, the ghosts were a nice change from the bugs, which smelt unpleasant.

As soon as I was out of hospital I received a request from Sydney to lead a deputation to ask for better treatment for conscientious objectors. I drove a borrowed car to Canberra to interview the legislators.

The deputation called on Bishop Burgmann on the way down. He asked why I had come when I still found difficulty in standing up for long.

"Someone had to drive and my husband thought I should."

"Do you always do what your husband tells you?"

"Usually. It saves the trouble of thinking."

"Edna," the Bishop called to his wife, "I want you to listen to this."

Standing about Parliament House made me feel as though my inside was full of fish-hooks. I saw the Prime Minister but all he would talk about was my books. We interviewed ministers who were tremendously kind and helpful. The bill to provide better treatment for conscientious objectors was later tossed out in the Senate when only a few hoary conservatives had stayed awake for it.

We called in to report to the Bishop on the way back. I was anxious to catch my train, which left Sydney at two in the morning. "There's no rush," the Bishop objected. "You can average sixty all the way."

Without averaging sixty I caught my train. Thanks to our interest in conscientious objectors and to Roddy's starting a co-operative among the miners, the town became convinced that we must be German spies with a secret radio transmitter in the chimney, and when we didn't return after the holidays the rumour went round that we had been removed to a concentration camp.

We were in Laurieton. We had got our own way at last. And by the most despicable means. We had used influence. There was at this time a most unconventional Minister for Education, who heard from a friend in Head Office what we were about. He said at once that if Kylie wanted to write a book about—what was the place?—of course Rodd should have it. He simply said, "Let there be Rodds at Laurieton", and there were. Head Office was furious and rightly so.

Roddy went back to the town we were deserting to superintend the removal of our battered furniture. He claimed I was not well enough to go with him, but he had never forgotten a previous move when I packed up all his first editions and sent them to the auction by mistake.

At Maitland two days later he flung himself into the train going north, just as it left the platform. I was encouraging him to run faster. Once before I had seen him miss a train when the Greeks at a café had been farewelling him with milk-shakes and we had to wait three days for another train.

As soon as he had recovered his breath he said, "Wait till I tell you—there really was a ghost. I saw it. I was sleeping on the floor of the empty house when I woke up and went to the window. A dark figure was coming up the side path by the roses. And when I looked again it just wasn't there."

"It was probably someone snooping to see what they could steal. Forget it. Think of the peace and quiet—this little peaceful place at last!"

Chapter III

THE CHARMING DEFERENCE of George Webber, the mailman, first made us aware of the role we were to play in Laurieton. In the Hunter Valley teachers had no social standing. But George, huge and handsome, indicated we were royalty, of an unnatural fragility to be delivered undamaged. Years before, the little town had had a famous headmaster who had taught George and his generation, and the populace hoped that the new headmaster would be such another. The parents wanted their children to have what they wistfully called "a chance in life".

Other passengers might squeeze into the overloaded service car as best they could or even stand on the running board, but the new schoolmaster and his wife must have the best seat beside the driver. Later, I stood on the running board myself in a sweep of wind and moonlight letting the tourists have the seat, because by then George was our friend. But that first evening, twisting between the holes in the road around Left-hand Lake, we were more formal. George would stop at an isolated house and a child would run to the gate while he bestowed naked strings of saveloys.

"What is this, George?" I asked at last. "Does it always happen or is it just a Friday special?"

George gave me an uncertain look. Perhaps I might complain that he was delivering sausages from his wife's café? At the café he disembarked his passengers, at the post office his mail, and then we were driven on to his mother's house where all was arranged for us to stay until our furniture arrived. For years dear old Mrs Webber and I used to bake our Christmas cakes together. I would do the beating and stirring and she supervised the cooking in her oven. Her face was all little pink cushions of kindness, and her natural sweetness somehow flavoured the cakes.

Next morning the drama of Laurieton—there was always some stirring action in progress—unfolded with a rescue from a shipwreck. Up the estuary in procession came the snapper boats towing a steamer that had gone ashore, and there was excited peering through binoculars. We were too tired to take it in. We only wanted to see the school.

The main street frayed out when it reached the rise at the foot of the Big Brother and we crossed a little valley by a footpath behind the church through an orchard and a tangle of ferns and wild raspberries. There were deep ditches with plank bridges and we wondered about these until we realized later that Laurieton often had the highest rainfall in the State.

The school and its accompanying residence stood in a park-like expanse rimmed with huge trees in what we came to see was the social centre of the town. The school had been painted rust-colour and was ornamented with a board which read, "Erected in 1883", not a vintage year for schools. On the opposite corner was the Community Hall, of hand-cut red mahogany, constructed by Uncle Johnny Longworth, the owner of the timber mill. On the diagonal corner was the Church of England donated by Uncle Johnny, who was also churchwarden. Opposite the schoolhouse, on the road running down to the post office and the punt, were the houses of the Longworth family.

The school residence had been built for the famous Mr Debenham, who had lived there for twenty-eight years and had thirteen children. It fitted us the way an outsize in overcoats would fit a midget. In front there were four bedrooms with the usual wide verandas and a living-room. Then down four steps was a passage with an afterthought of bathroom and a lofty wing which had either been a church or the original schoolhouse. It was divided into laundry, pantry, breakfast-room, kitchen. In the rain— and it started to rain next day—a stream of water gushed from the stove and flowed across the kitchen floor and out of the back door.

The residence had been cleaned for us and an interesting pattern of footprints showed in a light layer of mud. Mrs Webber's daughter, Allie Bell, big and blonde as her brother George, came to do my cleaning until I was stronger. She sniffed when she saw the footprints, knowing which of her nieces had made them. She was a meticulous housekeeper, but I more appreciated her devilish sense of humour.

Great camphor-laurel trees shaded the house. There was a thicket of Chinese elms in which bantams perched, a bush-house full of ferns to which I added all kinds of rarities. There were clumps of perfumed pink lilies growing in the grass, naked ladies on tall red stems. Beside the veranda, running wild, were two sorts of cucumber, a little prickly mottled porcupine of a cucumber, good for salads, and a swollen great Germanic cucumber for pickling. There were tobacco plants by the tank, and old gentlemen would come in when tobacco was scarce to beg the leaves. Down at the end of the yard —which seemed to stretch for about a quarter of a mile—a periwinkle had escaped from a rockery and swarmed over an ever-enlarging territory towards the broken-down fowlhouse. We were dazzled with these discoveries and wished only to explore and savour them.

It had not occurred to us that by moving to the coast we would become more directly involved in the war, but our first task was to arrange blackout curtains for the enormous windows of the kitchen-church facing the sea. The night we moved in an ancient man came galloping up from the coast-watchers on the headland, swearing a light was showing from the back of the residence. We were brusque with the old fool; we crushed him. Then while we were showing him his error we found a fanlight, so high in the rafters above the back door we had not known it existed.

The snapper-boat men had been reporting appearances of a submarine to the local defence authorities and had been told that what they saw was a whale. This appealed to their sense of humour because their eyesight was so keen they could pick out the white fleck of the flag above their fish-trap from a thousand white-flecked waves. Also they were acquainted with whales. When they were ordered to take a dinghy out to sea to escape if their boats were sunk they had to lie on the grass to laugh. Anyone with good enough aim to pick off a snapper boat could also hit a dinghy.

The Returned Soldiers' League was busy with plans

against a Japanese landing. An air-raid shelter was to be constructed in the school playground and the children drilled to march into it. As the country was supplied with mountains that could swallow a regiment in one fold—the Comboyne Range was only ten miles away—the children would have all gone elsewhere, but the indispensable step for all town gatherings was taken. A barrel of beer rolled into our yard the first week-end that it was not raining. The population assembled about the beer-barrel and veterans of World War I went into conference.

Allie Bell and I had our own plan of defence. My part would be to stand at the back gate with cups of tea. "And besides me, Allie, *you* will be standing wearing my black nightdress. That should hold them!"

Allie touched her yellow curls. "I hear they like blondes," she said. She was at least the size of two Japanese, or maybe three, taking her all round.

Mr Hoschke, who in World War I had caught pneumonia in France guarding horses that some mad veteran of the Boer War had imported for a cavalry charge, was now planning our bomb refuge. It was a replica of the best and deepest trench ever dug on French soil. It zigzagged. It was protected from cross-fire by rifles. There were redoubts for infantrymen. It was floored with duckboards, lined with pit-props, roofed. There were sandbags piled on top and it looked as though some immense animal had been burrowing.

The air force roaming up and down the coast used it as a landmark and practised strafing it. The children, drilled to a hair, could assemble and march into that trench five minutes after the planes had passed over and were far up the coast. In the rain it formed a natural reservoir of yellow mud and water, and no threats of punishment could keep the boys out of it. The trench took two week-ends to dig and five years for the headmaster and bigger boys to dismantle and fill it in. The headmaster's face when it saw it was as interesting a study as the trench.

Not to be outdone, the women of the town were there, pasting every window in the school with strips of linen soaked in evil-smelling glue. When one of the buildings was pulled down years later we had still not managed to remove the anti-shatter device. And we'd tried everything.

Then there was the first-aid class of which I was, undeservedly, the star. My reputation arose when Allie Bell and a stout, dark friend took me oystering to the Hope— a salt lagoon where the coastguards' houses lay between the surf and the sea-wall. This lake had been the original river entrance, but when the breakwater was constructed the river was given a new channel between stone walls half a mile long. The Hope was cut off to one side and was occupied by black swans.

On the way back along the breakwater Allie's friend put her foot on a loose boulder and rolled down to the water's edge, gashing her leg and dislocating her ankle. Without thinking I pushed the hideously protruding ankle-bone back into place, bound the cut under the knee with my scarf and ran to the nearest houses at Dunbogan for a boat. The man who rowed the boat thought it was all a great joke and had a most flirtatious conversation with Allie's friend.

But apparently I had done something very clever without thinking. It was agreed that the first-aid equipment should be kept at the school. I always cringed at the possibility that I might be expected to use the catgut in a jar of alcohol to stitch someone up. Bearers would appear at the door on occasion with some broken-limbed sufferer to watch me put on splints while someone else went for a car to take the victim to doctor and hospital thirty-five miles away at Port Macquarie. The doctor came usually once a week to see patients in a gloomy annex to the Community Hall.

Putting on splints was not as worrying as coming home and finding a trail of blood leading up to the back door and then away again. Or having a breathless message: "Come quick! The butcher was drunk again and he's chopped his hand with the cleaver." With supreme cunning I managed to use sticking-plaster instead of the needles and catgut to repair the butcher. When I nearly chopped one finger off myself with a reaping hook I treated the cut in the same way and, although the bone was showing, the finger was as good as ever.

The class in first-aid never did receive its certificates because the examiner was drunk both nights that we waited for him. The class disbanded.

To add to the effect of an abandoned battlefield at the school workmen arrived and began to tear down the church-kitchen. They tramped cheerfully on the roof while I typed. Walls crashed down around me. We could not ever find out if this was revenge on the part of Head Office or whether the Building Branch, interested by the scandal of Roddy's appointment, had turned up the files and found that repairs to the residence had been ordered twenty years earlier and never carried out.

By that time the first wave of visitors who stayed overnight or for a couple of weeks as the fancy took them had begun to arrive. There were also what we called Ruinlookers who acted on the principle of the English peer who told the poet, "Seeing there are no ruins in your country, Mr Longfellow, I thought I would visit *you.*"

Roddy tiptoed back to bed at dawn once—the lavatory was an isolated structure and the path through wet grass was favoured by enormous spiders that constructed webs the size of a fishing net—and said he had circled round by the side veranda where a Ruin-looker was occupying a stretcher amid displaced household furniture and rolls of linoleum.

"I am always suspicious," Roddy said, "of a man who sits up writing poetry before sunrise with nothing on but a holy medal." It was this Ruin-looker, when he and I were riding out to the beach, who told me that we were not alone. "Theresa is always with me," he volunteered. It turned out the invisible Theresa was a character in his novel.

"Theresa is always with me," Roddy would murmur when he found me digging the vegetable garden instead of typing.

Roddy himself joined the walking wounded. The doctor talked knowledgeably about golf to my father when they paid us a simultaneous visit. He was more interested in my father's handicap and never did explain why Roddy had keeled over in a dead faint. Later, a specialist explained that he had seen plenty of cases like it. The heart was not affected but the nerves of the heart were. It was by and large the result of extreme physical exertion.

Roddy and the bigger boys had been constructing cement paths across the muddy waste from the school gates to the school. The children walked long distances round the foot of the mountain, up from the satellite villages of North Haven and Dunbogan on either side of the channel. They came in boats down the lake. When tempests blew up and the wind and the current were so strong that the punt couldn't take the Dunbogan children across the river, a snapper boat would put in at the wharf and Roddy would see the children safely aboard.

They used to sit all day in the freezing schoolhouse with wet feet until we found out, then a row of socks drying in front of the school fire while they worked was not uncommon. The Department refused to provide cement paths through the quagmire leading from the gates so the teacher and boys built them.

They also repaired the swimming pool near the mill. Roddy was most adroit at pile-driving. Every child learnt to swim. It was a fishing town, yet this was quite a novelty. In a long, straggling line they would set off, climbing stiles and fences, circling round the mill dam. As the girls were supposed to be chaperoned I had many a reluctant swim in the weedy baths until Roddy enlisted the help of Peg Slocombe, who loved to swim.

The workmen whom the Building Branch had forgotten continued to pull the house down and hated to leave. Every man of them was a keen fisherman so the job took as long as possible. Also they knew that Manpower was going to seize them as soon as the job was finished. While they were all away fishing someone stole the new bath which was lying in the back yard. Timbers and roofing mysteriously vanished.

Then there was a frightful row between a building inspector and the foreman and they all packed their tools and went away, leaving me still cooking in the front bedroom. When after what seemed years a couple came back and replaced my charming church by a small kitchen, bathroom and back veranda, we thought we could settle to that peace which had vanished like some distant, laughable dream.

Chapter IV

Ernie, in the bright early morning, waited for Sam to bring the punt across, and while he waited admired the Macgregors' garden in a slip of land between their oyster lease and the punt wharf. This tiny allotment was right on the edge of the mangroves and the beds were built up full of seaweed, the weatherboard shack held together with vines and climbing pumpkins. There was a kind of arbour of tomatoes. Lettuce the size of cauliflowers with complicated frills, white onions the size of plates, were grown by the two quiet elderly bachelors. Not an inch of space was wasted, not a weed was there. If a plant in the back row showed signs of laziness a Macgregor would advance on it with a hoe and that plant sat up and improved.

As Ernie regarded the Macgregor garden dim landowning ancestors stirred in his blood. It was then he formed the ambition to one day grow onions equal to the Macgregors'. Of course he never did, but the poison of agriculture had entered his mind, hitherto more occupied with politics, horse-riding and mining.

Crossing to the Dunbogan side, he turned left behind

Uncle Johnny Longworth's house with its windmill above the water trough and the racecourse as a kind of back paddock. Here cows grazed and there were mushrooms in the rough grass. Ernie took the road along the lakeside, leaving the town on the opposite shore with the smoke from the timber mill lying like a fallen scarf around the mountain-foot. The town, in the early sunlight, was still rubbing the sleep from its eyes. Shags perched on grey piles and settled their neck feathers; oyster leases showed black sticks and numbered notices in the wide still water. Ahead on rising ground was thick scrub where the town girls went to pick a cartload of boronia whenever they wanted to decorate the Community Hall for a dance, throwing out the sweet-scented pink flowers next morning to wilt unregarded.

The track was heavy grey sand, for the seashore was only a quarter of a mile to his left and the murmur of it came over the sand-ridges. Across the creek was jungle country with staghorns and orchids in the tree crotches and black mud under the sulky wheels. Then the track ran out on the plains and Diamond Head swelled up in front with smooth green contours of turf tapering down to forest tops about its flanks. The sulky was going across the black peat land where Christmas bells flickered a rush of small flames in their woody-sounding bells. Far off towards the South Brother were a line of paperbarks advancing in decorative attitudes.

The great green haunch of Diamond Head sprawled out onto the beach with a little creek creeping out of its protection as if to taste the salt water. Diamond Head had another creek, with a golden lagoon on its southern side, draining the plains behind, which had once been all underseas when the river ran by Diamond Head. Gradually this entrance had silted up and the lake had shrunk inland until the strip of seven miles of sandy level cut it off from the ocean. The plain in a wet season still reverted to its former habit and became one great bog.

Ole Mammy, Blue and the Pup set their noses in the creek. The horse drank, blowing sensitively on the surface. By the beach there was an old ruined racecourse—Uncle Johnny's—and a couple of houses he had planned for holiday letting, which were in the lonely occupancy of white ants. Where the track curved round the rear of Diamond Head the paperbarks had new leaves the colour of red wine. Ernie noticed a fire had gone through here, singeing black the outer bark above the torn strips of pink, white and buff inner bark. It was always dark and shady in the patch of forest with lawyer vines tangled in the trees. Then there was a great stand of redgums near the Metcalfe gate and beyond, on the rise, the cleared land cheerful in broad sun with the homestead, the old fig-tree, the grape trellis, orchard and beehives.

His brother Jack helped Ernie unload and Clara, his sister, put the kettle on while Ernie was restoring the pup to Ole Mammy and taking the horse out of the shafts. Ernie had a look at the pig and scratched under its ear. He asked how the bees were doing and was told they were in bloody poor shape. All the Metcalfes were great beekeepers. Presently the three of them, Jack, Clara and the wanderer, were eating Clara's good cake, sitting round the kitchen table.

Clara was a woman with a gentle smile and an active domestic mind. When she was seventy-five she walked to Laurieton to see the doctor and he told her that he wished he could be as fit as she was. She could climb the cliffs, at that age, better than I could. She held the half-share of the farm that had belonged to her mother, and Jack owned the other half-share. Jack Metcalfe was the youngest of the family and was born of a different father. He was a worrier—always had been.

He had a stubborn bullock's face and head, he was cantankerous, and strangely enough bore the reputation of being a great lady's man. Now, with Ernie home, he complained of pains in his chest, his bad heart. Diamond Head was killing him. Clara had saved up enough money to build a new house because, she said, this one was so eaten with white ants it was likely to fall down. Besides, she said, the place was too "shut in", and where her new house would stand you could see over the open paddocks to the peak of the South Brother against the sunset. Clara had always been a great one for sunsets and her brothers teased her.

"The trouble with you," Ernie asserted, his mouth full of cake-crumbs, "is that you don't settle down. The family that was here before moved from over where you want this house built because they said it was too lonely and they liked to be near the road to see the traffic going by. They might miss something. And now after only about twenty years you've got to move back. I suppose it's all this traffic whirling past."

Jack had a literal mind. "Might be a car come by sometimes—chaps fishing. Get bogged in the wet, but."

"You're a fine one to talk, Ernie." His sister smiled. She was glad to have him home and it was her habit to wait on people. Jack gave her not enough scope.

Athol Stace came out to build his mother-in-law's new house. Jack plodded and complained. Ernie was the most deft and daring, joking as he straddled the roof. It was a four-room cottage and, with materials hard to come by, was made of grey fibro with a corrugated-iron roof. It was fenced all around so that the cows should not eat Clara's roses or the grape cuttings she brought from the old place. Behind it was the track up to the cliffs and in front the ploughed land and paddocks stretched away rimmed with trees. On a slope Jack had planted corn and on the other side was the vegetable garden, the fowl-house.

Ernie began dismantling the old house and carting the great slabs of red mahogany that constituted the walls to make a barn which stood more solid-seeming than the new house. His attention was taken by the little lake beyond the pasture and he would walk down in the evenings to study it. Fish swam up from the sea between the ferns and tree-roots and the blue water-lilies. Diamond Head held this lake, curled round it as though it were a golden cup it guarded, holding it between two paws of and.

"A man," Ernie said, "could drain that lake."

"You're mad," Jack replied with the true Metcalfe impulse to disagree with a brother.

"You'd get another acre of good grazing."

"And kill your bloody self into the bargain. It'd take a dozen men and a team of horses and then you wouldn't bloody do it."

"A man could do it on his own." Ernie had been growing restless.

The South Brother heaved itself up against the sunset as the pig heaved itself against the fence when Ernie went to talk to it in the evening. But the South Brother was only a tame peak and Ernie's thoughts were of gold and sapphires in the Great Dividing Range. He still wore his boots of Queensland leather and had sworn to go back to

Queensland when they wore out. Twenty-five years later they had still not worn out.

Diamond Head, true to its uncanny character, offered to all who came to it what they most cared for. What Ernie most cared for was a stupendous task, a problem to solve, something that no other man would undertake. Diamond Head held out the lure of the lake.

It was Jack the worrier who noticed the lump under Ernie's chin and found out he had another on his lip. Ernie claimed he was putting ointment on them, but to stop Jack's nagging he agreed to go to the doctor in Taree, forty miles south, a town with a big hospital.

Ernie made light of the whole affair. The milk truck would call for him on Monday and he'd have a rest in hospital after all this work. They'd just worn him out with building this house.

"Why didn't you tell us before?" Clara demanded, and Ernie said that if a man began to worry about a lump on his jaw he'd start letting her fuss over him and the next thing he knew she'd have married him off to some poor unfortunate woman the way she'd always planned. When Ernie went off to hospital with his clean-washed pyjamas in a little case such as children use for school books his sister sat down and cried.

"He knew it was cancer," she said to Jack. "He never let on."

The nurses made a great pet of Ernie because he was handsome and good-humoured. They asked which one of them he would marry and he laughed, saying that no woman could catch him because he could run faster than any girl.

"Be-the-gawd," Jack said later, "the doctors damn near cut his head off. He'd uv been dead if he hadn't uv went."

Ernie grew a piratical beard and moustache and hid the scars. He dreamt of his little lake with blue water-lilies in the shadow of the trees. When he came home he bought Jack's half-share of the farm, for he still had a money belt from his Queensland gold-mining. Jack wanted two hundred pounds, which was what the whole farm cost originally, and he retired to Laurieton to nurse his bad heart. He had a war pension of £1 6s. 3d. a fortnight and established himself on the sawdust dump in a beautifully fitted cedar caravan under a great fig-tree. He was within walking distance of the hotel. He could watch the "outside" fishermen load their lobster traps and the "inside" fishermen drying their nets. He could stroll across to Dot's house for a cooked meal when he felt like it. Clara worried about him and felt he had not long to live. That was why she had persuaded Ernie to take over the farm.

When Jack was over eighty he was still disparaging Ernie's farming.

"Before I left I ploughed the paddick. I left the furrers open. 'All you got to do,' I says to him, 'is put in the fertilizer with the bean seeds and push the dirt in on top.'

" 'Why?' he says.

" 'Why,' I says, 'because that's the bloody way they go in.'

"He *poked* them in. No fertilizer.

" 'How'd the beans go?' I says to him later.

" 'Bloody eel-worms ate 'em,' he says. Eel-worms!"

Chapter V

Ernie's grandfather, the Welsh poacher who was transported for taking a pheasant, had a son, John Metcalfe, who was a bullock driver with a farm up in the ranges out from Walcha. In the high tablelands the people are as hard as the grey granite boulders that once made good cover for bushrangers. Possibly the convict grandfather came to Port Macquarie, for his son carted stores between the Port and Walcha, a hundred miles up through the ranges that would break a man's heart as well as a bullock's: slow, hot sunbeaten miles, walking beside the team, sweat and effort getting them over the pinches, the strain of the heavy load, the lonely camp.

At the end of the trip John Metcalfe would throw his cheque on the bar counter and drink it out. His wife, Frances, had to go round the stations sewing, and she was also a midwife. Her first child, Harry, was born under the bullock dray. Her family increased to six boys and four girls and, apart from one little girl who was drowned, they all throve. Ernie often spoke of "The Mother" as one speaks of a deity, but of his father he never spoke at all.

His elder brother George left home at the age of eleven and found himself a job in a timber mill. The father never made any inquiry after him. Some time later the man rode past and called to his son: "Hear you've got a job?"

"Yes."

"See you keep it then." And he rode on.

Clara, as the eldest girl, managed the house and the little ones while The Mother would be away awaiting the arrival of a baby on some grim farm. Clara was ten when Ernie was born on 21st September 1885, and she reared him. She never lost her habit of caring for the family. But it was a miracle Ernie ever grew up because he could think of more devilment than other boys. He sought out snakes and would pick them up and crack them like a whip.

"He was a bugger for snakes," Jack recalled. Jack detested snakes. "He'd bring them home—tiger snakes, black ones, brown ones. Once he sent me for the shovel and the womenfolk see me going off with it. 'What d'you want the shovel for?' they asked. 'Ernie wants to dig out a snake.'"

The outcry women made over little things like that or boys falling off bucking horses or out of trees formed a habit in Ernie of "never letting on" when he was badly hurt. He would stagger home somehow and not let the girls know.

"Clara spoilt him," Jack said morosely. "He was The Mother's favourite, too."

Jack, the youngest, tagged along when Ernie truanted. "Your boys weren't at school yesterday, Mrs Metcalfe." But how could a woman with a living to earn see that they got their schooling? Ernie was caned and thrashed and detested school the more. Then there came a schoolmaster who discovered the boy was brilliant and tried to persuade him to study for a scholarship. How could he let his mother work to keep him?

He was a born musician and could play any instrument. ("I always fancied a fiddle.") But his musician's hands broadened and became scarred with hard work. He was the lightest and gayest of dancers. One night he looked through the window of the wooden hall where drunken young men stumbled with flushed girls. "How stupid they look!" he said remotely. "I will never dance again." And he never did.

He would make these sudden decisions and keep them. For instance, he would decide not to drink for a space of so many years. He always kept to his word. He had a Spartan, ascetic streak and decided never to marry. He had observed married people.

Ernie said that what turned him off marriage was a neighbour's wife who was so fat she hardly stirred from her chair. She kept her husband's bullock whip by her and would flick it round the ankles of her children into any corner of the one-roomed hut. When he was a little fellow Ernie would be sent on a message and watch the woman through a crack in the door, fearful that she might lay that whip around his legs.

Clara married Bert Bullen, who had a pretty sister, Bertha Bullen. Ernie, Clara said, might have married her, but there was some misunderstanding. He thought she had not answered a letter he wrote her and he vowed never to write again. So Bertha married another man and Ernie went on his travels. He took good care to stay away, Clara said, until Bertha was married. "When Ernie went to the war Bertha cried for him. Married as she was, she wept for Ernie, and perhaps she was not the only one."

But Ernie, not grieving for his lost romance, went down the Darling in a canoe with another fellow, getting lost in the Menindee swamps, swapping fish for flour and tea at the stations. They were once taken for river pirates. They were often hungry, but they followed the Darling to the Murray River and the Murray to the sea across a quarter of the continent.

At this time Ernie's elder brother George had taken up a farm on the road that led from Moorlands to Diamond Head. He had become George-with-one-arm. George had lost the other arm working in the timber on Langley's Line—steep country where you rode on the logs down the mountain. George had put the new hand on the brake as it was at the back, the safest place. He was up in front and the new hand lost his head, let the logs gain speed. George was thrown off and his arm was crushed. "No compensation in them days," his son Harry said. So George cleared the farm and rode a white stallion that no one else could handle. Ernie said he once went to give old George some help but he couldn't work his pace. "I had to sleep in the sun for a week to recover."

George-with-one-arm wrote home that the family who had taken up land on Diamond Head wanted to sell their farm. The boys should buy it and make a home for The Mother. Ernie's brother Albert and Clara's husband, Bert Bullen, rode their push-bikes down the odd hundred miles to George's farm. Next door to him George had an Italian family growing grapes and the young men from the highlands of bitter grass and grey stone gaped at the fertility of the soil. In those days the North Coast was being opened up, all sunlit promise and prosperity, rich in dairy cattle and deep crops.

"Bananas," Albert said. "If you cleared that jungle you

could grow bananas. Sheltered from the southerlies and the frosts. Or you could try passionfruit."

They cycled over to Diamond Head with its crest to the sea and its tail of forest. The enchantment took them. Only time reveals the character of Diamond Head. The Pullens —their name seemed a good omen, being close to Bullen— welcomed the boys as their chance to get away. Why did they want to go? Well, the women found it a bit lonely. The children needed schooling. The Pullens promised to leave the whaleboat on the pebble beach below the cliffs. They spoke of the run of mullet on the beaches, showed the groper and lobster holes for fish-traps. If you wanted moorhen or duck you only had to shoot them on your own lake. There were plenty of kangaroos if you ran out of meat for the dogs. You could take a cart down on the beach and shovel up the pipis, boiling bucketfuls at a time for fowl feed. Wonderful golden eggs the hens laid when fed on pipi meat.

There were fields of maize and the orchard was coming into bearing. The Pullens had moved over to the road so they could put up a store and sell everything from tinned milk to sandshoes because the place was going to be a great holiday resort. Already Johnny Longworth had put up two houses and made a racecourse. People came and camped there for the races. ("I never ever won a race," old John Longworth said. "The jocks used to bet against my horses when they rode them.")

The Pullens wanted two hundred pounds for this valuable holiday resort. In 1913, two hundred pounds was a lot of money. But for three hundred acres freehold, with two hundred more on leasehold, it was still a good offer. The only one of the boys who had any money was Jack, who was seventeen at the time. His mother took his money because she said he would only waste it. He had been working a tin lease out from Tingha—"camped in the scrub miles from anywhere", Jack lamented. But he had a dispute over water rights and, the lawsuit going against him, he took a job at the smelting works.

The Mother put her savings to Jack's and bought "Dimandead", and it was a good thing she did because she never trusted banks and kept her money in a secret place in the house. They might not even have moved then, but one night when Jack was skating at a rink in the town men came yelling, "Jack, your bloody house is burning down." Everything was lost. The house was of cedar with cypress-pine posts and it burnt as though it was doing it for a bet. The skillion kitchen had mosquito net over the window to keep out flies and the lamp had caught it.

Jack had nineteen pounds and a diamond of one and a half carats from a claim he had staked. He sold the diamond to pay for the move to the coast. The Pullens had left with the blind haste of refugees.

Little by little after the Metcalfe family settled in they began to realize what Diamond Head was really like. You are living in the same cage as something uncanny and of unearthly strength. It is not the loneliness, the wild storms, the feeling of being cut off from humanity. It is the sense that Diamond Head is waiting to break you. It waits. It uses a man's own rush to throw him. It has tricks, not just to pick off some solitary fisherman from the rocks, but it seems to study out how to deal with men, find out their weaknesses.

The Metcalfe weakness was that they fought among themselves. Jack went off to the war in 1914, leaving the place to Albert after a fierce quarrel. Ernie, the best-tempered of men, came to take Jack's place, but he couldn't stand Albert either. Ernie lived on the farm but worked on the railway which was struggling through the swamps and mountains along the North Coast, much beset with rain and treacherous ground.

Ernie could have been a ganger because he had a marvellous eye for levels, but he preferred to be a navvy. ("The navvy is the gentleman of the working classes.") As a ganger he would have been excluded from the easy friendship of his fellows. He would walk the few miles across the plains to the lake at Humbug Bay where the Twomeys had a cottage. The Twomeys also worked on the railway and they would take a boat up the river to the rail camp. In the evening they came back the same way after a hard day's work and Ernie would often run the miles home to keep himself in training.

But Albert was unkind to the horses and Ernie had always treated animals as friends. They would follow him about hoping for a word and he talked to them as though they were people. Albert wanted the horses to recognize him as master. So Ernie spoke plainly to Albert and left to join Jack in France.

"I told him not to come," Jack said. "I writ and said, 'This is a bastard of a place.' It was about the time Hughes tried to bring in conscription and the officers wanted us to vote for it and we wouldn't. Be-the-gawd, didn't they pay us out! We'd be so tired walking round a shell-hole we'd fall in."

When Ernie caught up with Jack he told his brother for the first time in his life he was right about something. It *was* a bastard of a place. Jack was in hospital badly gassed and Ernie, more lightly gassed, overtook him there.

"It was our own gas," Jack explained. "Chlorine—phosgene. We sent it over, but the wind came up and blew it back. A good few died. Some blokes never even got their helmets on. They went sort of delirious."

A doctor had seen Jack at the back of the trenches and pronounced him dead. An orderly, by mistake, moved him to hospital where they said he would never get over it. Then another doctor told him, "You'll be able to swing the lead on this for six months."

After a few weeks in hospital he was back in the trenches and was wounded. He was two years in the trenches and shipped home, he said, a total wreck. When he was over eighty he felt that only coming of a long-lived family and drinking plenty of beer had preserved his life thus far.

Ernie never complained. His good humour kept his mates cheerful and when the bullets came like bees swarming he went forward a little surprised but not afraid. He enjoyed what there was to enjoy, remembering especially a pretty French girl in a ruined town who thought as little of marriage as he did. Returned from the war completely unharmed, he took up a soldier-settlement block on the irrigation area near that river he had once braved in a frail canoe. He grew great golden apricots, built himself a neat house which he kept scrupulously clean. He played a good game of tennis after working at back-breaking labour in the orchard. It was not the drought that beat soldier-settlers but the flourishing condition of their orchards. You could not sell apricots. There were so many that it was not worth shipping them to market. The banks foreclosed on the farms, the soldiers were evicted and the farms were bought by men who made fortunes out of them. Ernie walked off his property saying that he was fish-hungry and he could do with some surfing. He came back to Diamond Head and fished and surfed until even he was exhausted. Then he had the inevitable row with Albert over the way he treated the horses and went off to Queensland.

The one who missed Ernie most was Clara's boy, Bert. Clara had a shop in a Sydney suburb and Bert came to Diamond Head for the holidays. In those days it was under cultivation, fields of corn and crops, cabbages, tomatoes, vineyards. They would kill a goat, salt it down, fish with plugs of dynamite in the holes under the cliff, get a chaff-bag full, and smoke the fish in a home-built smokehouse. The fish would come in on the high tide, and at the new moon there were two high tides close together and the fish, knowing this, would remain in the holes. Under the flare of the lights they would panic and rush for the ledges. You could scoop them out with your bare hands. And then—a great piece of luck for Bert—one holiday he broke his arm and had to stay at Diamond Head, missing a whole term. He had been playing with other boys at Harry Metcalfe's farm and Bert was the wounded steer with horns tied on who rushed the other boys to gore them. He jumped at the fence, fell over it and broke his arm.

He never did catch up on his schooling and made an ample fortune. His great dream was to get back to Diamond Head and it followed him all his life. He worshipped Ernie. Ernie told him that some day they would build a boat and sail around the islands. They would take the rifle. They would go off together roving and seeing strange places. But Ernie went off alone to Queensland and Bert had to go back to his mother's shop.

There were some mighty queer things doing at Diamond Head after The Mother died in 1933. Jack complained that Albert was doing everything against him and the town of Laurieton claimed that the brothers had a still. "There were eighteen gallons of honey-beer for a wedding," Jack admitted. "And I said to Albert, 'There will be no more honey-beer made on these premises while I am here.'"

Then there were the nine gallons of honey-beer at a sale up on the Moorlands road where people were bewildered to find they had bought horses when they couldn't remember bidding for them, and Jack woke up with a lump on his head in the dairy where he slipped while carrying a demijohn. He didn't come to properly until the following morning. This time it was Albert who left. He took his bees and joined a little colony of invalid pensioners living under the cliff at Point Perpendicular. Their children used to walk to school and Albert, whose manners were always courtly to the point of magnificence, used to come into town to the hotel. On the way he would jut his beautiful white moustache over the fence to advise me about my bees and he would always come in to help me rob them. I would slip him ten shillings for this and no man ever received this sum with a better grace.

Clara had come up from Sydney when Jack was at Diamond Head on his own. She intended to pull the property together and she did. It was Clara who wrote the letter to Queensland telling of Jack's bad heart and how he was not expected to live much longer.

When Ernie came out of hospital differences developed between him and Jack, who expected Ernie to go in to Laurieton and sell farm produce from door to door.

"He was a very conceited bugger," Jack said later. "Him and Albert was always selfish. They hated selling anything. Give it away sooner. They'd go as far as the gate and invent any excuse to come back. Say they'd forgotten their tobaccer. Didn't like to call at people's doors and ask did they want anything." Ernie always disliked shopkeepers, but not as much as he detested "bosses". "You'd have thought selling was a crime. Always conceited and it made me damned wild."

Fewer and fewer people came to Diamond Head now that Uncle Johnny no longer held picnic races and the road was never repaired. Uncle Johnny had long ago given up Diamond Head as a bad job. "Too isolated," he told us. "Nothing does well there." Instead he let cottages in Laurieton where he could keep his eye on them. Uncle Johnny had a magnificent instinct for property.

Clara might have remained at Diamond Head with Ernie if it had not been for the argument over the pig. Clara had decided to kill the pig for Christmas and she always got her own way in a sweet womanly fashion. Ernie made a great scene about it.

"Go down and shoot my best friend!" He turned fiercely to a small red-headed great-nephew who was staying with them. "You'd better get inside before she wants me to shoot you, too!" He brooded over the murder of the pig in a way that Clara felt was quite unreasonable. Before she left she gave the best of the poultry to her daughter Dot because Ernie would only let them roost in the trees and be eaten by foxes.

Clara went off to take care of her son Bert in Sydney and Ernie was left alone at Diamond Head.

The two gentlemen-in-exile, Albert and Jack, would sometimes meet at the Laurieton hotel. They might be speaking or they might not.

"I hear Ernie's out there on his own," Albert said to Jack, nursing a glass and gazing down the river.

"Serve him right. Conceited cow. He's no bloody good as a farmer."

"What's he doing then?"

"He's draining the bloody lake."

"Well, that'll kill him if Dimandead doesn't. I reckon," said Albert the philosopher, "that place is like a whopping great ant-lion. It waits for some silly ant to sit down near it and—snap!—it eats him. It's ate us and it'll eat Ernie."

"He always was a mad bugger," Jack growled. At last they had found something they agreed on.

Chapter VI

ERNIE was just on the edge of his reputation as "the mad hermit of Dimandead". When we first arrived I would see him trudging up from the punt in the rain, a sack over his shoulders, leading the horse with a cartload of cabbages. I would see him going home, the cabbages still unsold, the rain dripping off the brim of his wide felt hat. He came in to sell me a cabbage now and then. He was just a man with a beard who was related in some way to that courteous old Albert Metcalfe who was so good with bees.

Then once when he came in with a cabbage I pointed out gently that I had a vegetable garden and was giving the vegetables away. He did not come again and I developed feelings of guilt. How mean can you be? I could have bought his cabbage and fed it to the fowls. It was only sixpence. I used to look out hoping that he would stop, but he never did. He was, as Jack said, too proud.

The endless procession of natives bearing gifts was wearing me down. If we went off for the week-end camping with the two horses we had bought, we would return to find a fisherman had walked into the kitchen and left a couple of fish on the kitchen table, a shy child had left a brown-paper bag of mushrooms. Someone had left a cake, a bucketful of crab legs.

We never locked a door and, although the Laurietonians were supposed to be great thieves, in the eleven years nobody stole anything but my drake and that was taken by some American airmen who had crashed their flying-boat in the river. Who would steal books? Or a typewriter? To the older people reading for pleasure was sinful—a waste of time when you could be working. Dancing was sinful and led inevitably to sexual intercourse. The primitive Christians who had come through with the bullock waggons had left their mark.

Farmers in the early days, burning down the great cedar forests and clearing "scrub" of valuable softwoods, had pondered on sin on their lonely farms. Their descendants never did become accustomed to my habit of talking to men. What was worse, my husband didn't seem to mind that I went out on the snapper boats with two men, one of whom had six children. I could also be seen painting and puttying on the boat-slip where Eddie Dobson was building a snapper boat, and this was worse because Eddie Dobson was a married man with eight children. Eddie, who knew his Laurieton, decided to bring his wife, Dot, down from the farm to chaperon him, and Dot proved so useful that she stayed on.

Eddie found that no more tools were stolen, accounts were kept, timber was delivered. Dot steered the snapper boat to Sydney through a howling gale towing a disabled timber boat while Eddie was seasick. Dot was so grateful to me that she always sent one of the children in with her special sweet biscuits.

Roddy took the senior pupils out to Eddie Dobson's

farm behind the Big Brother so that Eddie could show them the rare softwoods that grew in the gullies. The school collection of timber samples soon rivalled that of a technical museum as the men from the timber mill took an interest and brought in specimens. The boys polished them, labelled them with the correct names and hung them on the wall. Eddie came in to lecture on these wood samples.

"Those boys," he said, "had me gallied. Maybe I was a little careless when they were all saying, out at the farm, 'What's this? What's this?' but they'd gone back and looked all those wood chips up in a great thundering book on timbers. They had me on toast. 'Why did you say it was rosewood? The book says it isn't.' They kept me hopping."

When I gave Eddie a copy of the novel I wrote about Laurieton, *Lost Haven*, he read it aloud to his family at night sitting round the great open fireplace. "When I came to me own death," he said, "the tears was running down me face and I couldn't go on for crying."

It took some time for the parents to realize that the schoolmaster was teaching the children they must not kill the birds and animals. The first surprise had been that he did not cane the children, but this was excused because he "was bringing them on real well". Then he announced that anybody shooting satin-birds within a mile of the school would have him to deal with. They were protected. When asked who was protecting them he said, "I am." The area for a mile around the school was a bird sanctuary. He confiscated shanghais. And he became really ferocious when he came on two boys setting their dogs on a wombat, a slow, gentle animal. To the fishermen who shot swamp wallabies for bait in the fish-traps, and black swans to eat, who scraped the eggs from the female lobsters so that they could send them to market, this concern for animals and birds was comical.

I asked old Pop Slocombe about the corkwood pigeons which local families made into pies. Half an hour after our conversation shots rang out in the street behind the school. Pop came in beaming with a rifle in his hand and a bunch of dangling birds in the other. "There you are," he said generously. "Just enough to make a good pie." And I had to pluck them and cook them. Without their feathers they were about the size of a sparrow.

His daughters, Peg and Pat, became our great friends. Pat kept the hairdresser's shop and had a devoted admirer, Hughie McCafferty, who was a Presbyterian while the Slocombes were one of the few Roman Catholic families in the town. Peg had no fixed admirer at the time and she came riding with us. She tended the Catholic church and was altar boy when no one else came. She said she had found the linoleum in the sanctuary was really cream with a pattern. Until she scrubbed it when the cleaner was away she had always thought it was brown.

The Slocombes lived opposite the hotel which they had formerly leased and Peg's mother, Selina, knew more about what went on in the town than anyone else. I used to sit on her front veranda with her and she told me stories of great banquets in bigger hotels. The Slocombes had retired, but Selina had a grievance about the way the family had been ousted from their lease and kept watch on the hotel as an enemy fortress. The house was immaculate and the garden so well tended by Pop that his papaws positively shone. He had a jabiru stork in the garden which was the terror of fruit-stealing boys. It died mysteriously. How would you poison a stork? Its grieving owner put up a plaster stork by the bird-bath as a memorial. Pop Slocombe was a great adviser about horses and his tragedy was that when a flood came over the property he owned farther up the coast he had to stand on the upstairs veranda and watch his racehorses swimming around until they were drowned. I don't think he ever quite recovered.

We had bought two horses as the roads were too rough for a car and we could see the country on horseback. Creamy, Roddy's horse, never took any notice of her rider. She would dawdle about while the other horses went on, then, finding herself alone, she would throw up her head with a scream like a panic-stricken steam-engine and gallop off to rejoin her mates. Her rider clung on desperately. Coming home all the horses galloped—my brown Betty, Peg's piebald Freckles, with fat Creamy in the lead. They knew there would be a hot mash and their coats on against the cold. Once while I was stirring the mash Creamy gently fastened her teeth in the seat of my riding pants. She could jump any fence and then undo the gate to let the other horses in.

I would leap out of a sound sleep in the middle of the night with a cry, "The horses are in the garden", and there they would be. Creamy staked herself jumping a six-foot fence and Pop Slocombe showed me how to swab the wound and apply Stockholm tar daily. Anyone who has had to tend a suppurating wound behind a horse's foreleg until it heals will wonder why people ever keep horses. It is some kind of moral confidence trick horses have imposed on humanity. I had to rub them with kerosene for botflies. When Roddy was later taken to hospital with blood-poisoning and broke out in a mysterious rash at a time when doctors knew little about penicillin-allergy Pop Slocombe came up with an oozy, smelly grey mixture suitable for horses, and, sure enough, it cured the rash.

Dick Bibby, another friend, brought the milk. He would come riding past the fence after milking his cows in the evening and I would run out with the billy so that he need not get off his horse. He would tell me cruel old tales of timber-getters and bullock-drivers, wheezing with laughter as he came to where someone was hurt. He was as old and hard as a fence-post, a man nothing could destroy, and we were very fond of him. He kept our horses on his property by the lake when we went on holidays.

The horses were a great attraction at the school picnic when we went out past the Hope to a little lagoon by the pilot station. Every child had a ride along the beach at Point Perpendicular and everyone in the town who could came, whether they had children or not.

When we first arrived the boys fought all the time until Roddy produced a couple of pairs of boxing gloves and insisted that no fight should be without gloves or a referee. They soon took the measure of each other and the fighting stopped while they concentrated on bronze medallions for life saving. They were all very charming children.

There was one boy Roddy despaired of teaching anything. He called him over to the house for a talk.

"Jim," he asked, "what have you learnt this year?"

Jim thought. "I know two verses of 'The Lady of Shalott'," he said. "There's water in it."

"You always seem very tired?" Roddy queried.

"I go netting for bait at night," said Jim. "I earned sixteen pounds last week."

"I think you are wasting your time at school," said Roddy. "Get your mother to come up and sign a form. Then for the next nine months, until you are really old enough to leave, just put in an occasional appearance."

A couple of weeks later Jim put a grinning face in at the schoolroom window. "Earned twenty-eight pounds last week, Mr Rodd." When he was made a member of the crew of his father's snapper boat he met his former headmaster in the street. "I made sixty pounds for my share of the catch this week, Mr Rodd."

"Congratulations," said Roddy. "I don't make nearly that much."

Roddy would come over from the school and say, "I need a new play. Three good speaking parts for girls and two for boys. The rest to walk on with a few lines between them."

Everyone had to appear on the stage. This included one pretty girl who had had polio and had to sit down. It was easier to write the plays than to adapt others, and my English publisher, rather surprisingly, brought out the little books of plays in edition after edition. One play, *The Bushrangers' Christmas Eve*, has become something of a hardy annual in Australian schools.

When Roddy was persuaded by an enthusiastic inspector to take the children and put a play on at a teachers' conference in Taree a teacher in the audience grumbled, "It's all very well for Rodd with those bright children. I'd like to know the I.Q. of that girl who's taking the lead." Tracy, Rodd's assistant, leant over and said, "It may interest you to know that she hasn't got an intelligence quotient. She can't read and learns her part by hearing it repeated to her." The girl was an excellent mimic and could reproduce any gesture or even the intonation of my voice.

Once a month the school would straggle over to the Community Hall in an array of costumes. The duller the child the more it loved to have a part on the stage. All the mothers came and many of the fathers, paying a small coin which went to the school funds. How the children shone—the wild delight and pleasure of applause!

I was useful rehearsing and writing plays, but when it came to the sewing class, that was the school's weak point. It had been explained to me that either I taught sewing and was paid or one of the staff taught it unpaid. This mysterious ruling may still be in force. I was left-handed, but my mother-in-law taught me to sew right-handed before we came to Laurieton. I also fortified myself with a correspondence course on dressmaking, but the older girls borrowed it and were always ahead of me. There was an old relic of a sewing-machine. "Mrs Rodd, the sewing-machine won't go," some heavy-fisted child would report. I became an expert at repairing the sewing-machine. They all learnt to use it but, as they bought ready-made clothes, making their own was not very useful. They learnt embroidery stitches because I could embroider.

They never did learn to draft patterns because these completely bewildered me. I taught the class to sing part songs while we sewed. An inspector was puzzled: "They're all doing something different," he complained. "Why aren't they all sewing the same thing?" Some years later by some mysterious ruling a regular sewing teacher was appointed and every child lifted its needle at the same moment and in complete silence. The inspector loved it.

One pretty young assistant boarded with us. She just refused to find board elsewhere and moved in on us. Other teachers merely shared the midday meal because you couldn't see them munching a dry sandwich in the playground. Then later there were too many to feed and they had homes near by. Our boarder was very surprised when on her first afternoon, in the grey rain, we took her down to bring back my ducks from the mill-pond. They didn't want to come and the drake kept calling them out into deep water. I became impatient and plunged in fully clothed, swam out and herded them ashore. The ducks were as surprised as the assistant.

The drake was eaten by the airmen, who loved Laurieton and kept losing parts of their plane so that they would not have to leave. It was an inside job and I know which boys were in it—innocent, cherubic little fellows. One moonlight night the gang came up from the hotel, stole my drake and cooked it in the scrub. I only found the feathers. Three planes fell into our river during the war. One just cleared the roofs and presently I saw four people gesticulating and talking at the Guvmint Wharf at the foot of the street where a boat had put them ashore.

Roddy was chopping wood in the back yard when I came with the information, given by an excited girl, that the four were film stars on an entertainment tour. "There are two men," I reported. "One with a large moustache is called Jerry Colona and another is called Bob Hope."

"Never heard of them."

"Aren't you even going to look at them?"

"Why should I? Now if it was Dorothy Lamour I'd go and see her."

There was great glory for Laurieton and a dance at the Community Hall where the tired entertainers were kept up till two in the morning. We could hear the music across the street. Next day I received a telegram from a Sydney paper asking for special articles and "any exclusive information about Bob Hope". I wired back, "Have no exclusive information about Bob Hope", and walked over the top of the Big Brother to Eddie Dobson's farm to be out of the way.

The trouble with Laurieton was that there was too much happening all the time. If it wasn't castaways it was visitors or the confounded horses. Uncle Johnny Longworth and I used to ride up together seven miles to Kew to have them shod. His daughter said she liked to know I was with him when he went to get his horse shod because he was so very old and something might happen if he were alone.

Uncle Johnny, as a timber man, had a hatred of trees. He had lopped all the trees in the streets into green mops and the school, with huge trees all around it, made his fingers itch for an axe. He would go past and see me on the roof cleaning leaves out of the gutters.

"Want to get a boy to do that, Mrs Rodd."

"It's too dangerous, they might fall off."

"Trees—no good near a house. Rot the gutters. Branches fall down. Dangerous in storms. Ought to have all these trees cut down."

I might have known the old devil was planning something when he sent a message that he wouldn't be coming to the blacksmith's to have his horse shod. It always took most of the day. I would be towing Betty while I rode Creamy. Then you had to find the blacksmith. He had to open the smithy and heat his tools. On our way there one day Uncle Johnny and I rode past a bullock team hauling a log. The men had sat down by the roadside to boil the billy. It was probably Ace Crane, whose daughter was the ornament of my sewing class. His bullocks were not as badly knocked about as the whip-gashed teams from the Kendall mill that tourists thought were so picturesque. By the time we rode back the bushfire started by the bullock-drivers' fire had leapt the road and burnt its way to the top of the Big Brother where it flared until the next rainstorm.

On this day when Uncle Johnny cunningly stayed home I came plodding back in the afternoon and from far down the main street saw the gap in our fence trees. I let out a yell of rage. The great pine-tree had fallen in an explosion of boughs, one of which had shattered the bush-house above my orchids. The top of the tree was six inches from the residence gate, which wouldn't open.

"Why did you let him do it?"

"He was too quick for me," the headmaster explained. "I was teaching and he just popped his head round the door. 'That old dead pine,' he said. 'I brought my axe over. Have it down in no time.'" Roddy was really full of admiration. "You know, it was rather dangerous. No one else would have been game to climb up as he did." Uncle Johnny was seventy-eight when he shinned his way up that tall tree to put the guide line round the top of the trunk. It wasn't his fault it hadn't fallen clear of a great gum-tree.

A year later the white Saanen goats I had bought were still playing chasings up and down the trunk of the pine-tree. It was harder to get rid of than a stranded whale. Finally we paid Terry McGeary and his father to saw it into sections. The butt was as thick through as a cartwheel. The mill manager came and looked at it, but he wasn't interested in pinewood. "Nice bit of firewood," said the McGearys as they went off, leaving the great chunks. We were still at that time trying to burn off my church-kitchen which the builders had left stacked up in the back yard.

It was Uncle Johnny's passion for neat symmetrical arrangements that caused him on Sundays, when he was counting the money from the collection plate, to replace all sixpences and threepences with two-shilling pieces from his own pocket. He would arrange these on a little ledge round the plate. "Makes it easier to count, Mr Rodd," he would mutter to his fellow warden in the vestry.

Dear old Uncle Johnny had never been sure of Roddy's Christianity since, as lay reader, he had read the congregation Tolstoy's story, "How much land does a man need?" instead of a sermon. Uncle Johnny took it much the way Mrs Hoschke, a keen gardener, had taken our parson's Easter sermon on the beautiful white butterfly that emerged from its ugly chrysalis. "That was a cabbage moth," she hissed in my ear.

If Uncle Johnny, a laconic man, had been able to reply to Roddy, he might have done it like this and I would have sided with him:

"Mr Rodd, you are a clever man and well educated. You have read us the story of a man who ran himself to death trying to own more and more land until he died and needed only six foot of it. You and Tolstoy are saying that men should not be grasping and straining to own land. But what is Christianity if it does not teach a man to exert every effort and sinew, expressing himself in what he does best? And if you have a talent for acquiring land you might as well exercise it. Since when has land-owning become unrighteous? Is making a living such a poor thing? Is a milkman under a curse for taking the cow's milk? Is a butcher un-Christian? Or a man that tears down trees in a forest? Is he committing a sin? For every man that lives is, by breathing, depriving some other creature of breath. And all that lives lives on the flesh and blood of some other thing. So why should you come and disturb our minds by asking, 'How much land does a man need?'

"Ah, and the small bird in his bush will dart out to defend it, because it is his, and for his young to leave to them for ever. And you are talking of a dead man, Mr Rodd, when you say he needs but six feet of earth. A living man needs more. And that is the great debate. How much does a *living* man need, and his young—or maybe the tribe of townsfolk? How much does a city need? And it takes centuries to work that one out and get the sum wrong in the end. So that this is a question we shall maybe die of—and *then* you can talk of six feet of ground—not till then!"

And indeed no gentler man than Uncle Johnny ever went to his inheritance of six feet of earth. Once you try to eradicate the human urge for ownership the human race is done for, because this and being human are synonymous. Those who want no money or land still demand attention and the cry of, "Look at me, Lord!" goes up from every church. And very right, too.

Chapter VII

IT WAS A FEW MONTHS after we first arrived that Mrs Twomey, a handsome, stately woman from Humbug Bay, called to see what the new headmaster's wife was like. She brought a basket of rosellas to be made into jam, and later sold me a side of goat for Easter. The Sydney visitors, even when they knew what it was, found it delicious. She not only had a herd of goats but kept bees and invited me to visit her at her home far up the lake shore.

A week later old Pop Twomey came stamping in wanting to know which day he could call to take me to Humbug. He was a huge old man with stormy eyebrows and his thirteen children were settled all around the district. He immediately got into an argument with Roddy, who said that the same bee *could* sting you twice. He personally had been stung twice by the same bee. Pop roundly told him he did not believe him. Roddy said the bee had stung him on the foot and when he had gently picked it off so as not to break the barb it had stung him on the hand.

Pop obviously had doubts whether the school-teacher should be trusted near children. Nevertheless he repeated the invitation to Humbug and I rode out, leaving my horse for his granddaughters to ride during the Christmas holidays. The mare, after I left, bucked off the youngest granddaughter and went back to Moorlands to look at her colt, from which she had been removed far too soon by an unscrupulous dealer.

I made a worse impression on poor old Pop than my husband by asking if I might come out with him to watch him ring mullet. He was an "inside" fisherman who fished the lake rather than go "outside" with the snapper boats through the surf. Pop intended to go ringing mullet at midnight and it was raining hard. Fishermen always, depending on the tides, seem to go out at midnight or dawn or two in the morning. Pop was shocked by my request. He bluffly refused. What hurt him was that I did not seem to realize that he was a hale man of seventy-five. I was perfectly willing to trust myself with him in the boat. He was not sure which was most sinful—that I should make such a proposal or that I didn't realize what I had escaped. His wife tried to keep her face straight but he could see she was laughing.

Ma Twomey told me how to make a double-headed penny for playing two-up, which she had learnt when her husband was working on the railway—I think it was her first husband. She was living in the railway camp and all the men used to leave their money with her because nobody would steal from a woman. She advised me that a new hive should be wiped out with peach leaves because the bees liked the smell, and it was Mrs Twomey who first took me to Diamond Head.

When Pop went into town on Saturday morning in the car he dropped his wife and me off on the road across the plain and we walked over to visit Clara Metcalfe. The Metcalfes had just moved into their new house and the old one was still standing. We came up through the redgums to the gate I was to know so well—two sliprails fitted into posts—and as we went along the track shaded by tall trees I exclaimed with pleasure at the blue lilies on the lake.

Then a head emerged from the earth—curly hair going grey, a pointed beard, then the whole of Ernie in a grey flannel singlet and corduroy trousers held up with a leather harness strap, his brown arms like tree-roots, his navvy's shovel gleaming silver. The trench in which he had been standing was over six feet deep. He fell into step with us and explained he was draining the lake, but the roots were giving him trouble.

"Why are you draining it? It's so beautiful."

Ernie said, straight-faced, "I need the exercise. A man's got to do some little thing to keep fit."

There was a small red-headed great-nephew with Clara, so it must have been before the great pig argument. Indeed, I remember Ernie taking me to see the pig. The great-nephew, John, rode on Ernie's shoulder up to the cliffs, where the gill-birds were at their eternal fluting in the banksia combs and we stood to look far down the fifteen miles of beach to Crowdy Light, over the rocks, the beach lagoon, miles of scalloped surf, dunes, with the tangle of swamp and scrub behind them. When I had a septic jaw for three months from a local tooth extraction I used to imagine I was standing on the cliff looking south with the smell of pale wild violets coming up from the grass. We scrambled down the cliff and looked at all the drift thrown up by the storm, then circled back by the lagoon and the creek running into it, through tall she-oaks and wild hops with their pale green umbels.

Clara Metcalfe and Mrs Twomey were still drinking tea

and indulging in that allusive conversation of women who have been neighbours for years. They treated me indulgently, finding me interesting and harmless but not quite human. Ernie, of course, with his sympathy for strange animals, was at ease with me. He remembered, however, I was the wife of a school-teacher and for this breed he had a great antipathy.

The next time I came to Diamond Head I was riding down the coast with young Len Shoesmith, who had been given leave from school to act as guide over the fishermen's track to Crowdy Head. We would stay overnight and come back next day. Ahead of us waddled Len's stout old cattle-dog, Bill, who flushed out a snake just before my mare Betty put her foot on it. He chased it into the bushes, for he was a great snake-killer but slow with age. We did not see any death adders, though the scrub was reported to be alive with them.

We called at Diamond Head on our way out and Clara gave us cake and tea. Ernie showed us the short cut through the paperbarks by the creek to the trail across the plains going south. Nobody went that way any more. Indeed, Len and I often had to take to the beach.

Ernie stood to watch us, his brown felt hat over his eyes, under the shadow of the paperbarks. He blended so well, in his old grey flannel and corduroys, that you could not have seen him at any distance.

"Why don't you call in when you're in Laurieton and borrow some books?"

"I might do that."

He had always carried a book in his swag although book-reading was nothing that he had ever been encouraged to do.

On our way home Len and I did not call at Diamond

Head. There was a grey scud of cloud over the lonely farm and the horses were keen to be home. Len was telling me about his sister, whom I remembered meeting at Humbug, a wild dark girl on a fidgety horse. "She always rode with me," Len said. "Never any good in the house but good with horses." The two of them had been coming down the ranges when something frightened the girl's horse. It bolted down the road and round a corner and when Len urged his horse after it he turned the corner and found Gloria lying in the road dead. "I miss her," the boy said.

We were passing through the jungle behind the dunes and just then my horse shied and started to run, jarring my finger against the pommel. I could hardly hold her and after I reached home my finger swelled and swelled until I was wearing my teeth down grinding them with the pain. "A jealous ghost," I told Roddy.

"You and your ghosts!"

While I was in hospital overnight at Port Macquarie to have the finger cut open, Ernie called to borrow a book. Often people called to see me and made friends with my husband instead. Ernie and Roddy shared meals and books for years after that. Ernie said later that Dimandead might have licked him if it hadn't been for the books. The wind might be coming across the open paddocks nearly lifting the roof off Clara's house and flinging rain at it like insults, the seas would be roaring to lift the cliff, the radio battery would be flat. Ernie would go to bed and read, and let Dimandead do its worst.

Now, instead of going past our house, he would come in, shaking his waterproof at the back door, yelling "Anyone at home?" sure of his welcome, the books in his knapsack. In the next ten years he read his way steadily through our library. Fiction did not interest him as much as history and biography, but he read all Dickens, Tolstoy, and Balzac, as well as Roddy's collection of Polar and African explorers. If I were away he might stay overnight, playing chess with Roddy, sharing a bottle of wine. We did not realize he never went to the hotel because he could not afford to "shout". He was not too proud to wear Roddy's old coats, but he was too proud to accept a drink and not return it.

Roddy was a good cook and I had my own special dishes. We had one Christmas dinner together when I cooked a duck with red burgundy and we ate it looking down the blue water on the back veranda. Later at Diamond Head Ernie and Roddy shot a hare and jugged it in wine, but they didn't let it stand long. I was a little jealous of the easy way they had with each other. "Ernie, you old devil," Roddy would cry over the chessboard, "it's checkmate."

"No, it isn't," Ernie would tell him. "But if you move that piece you'll spoil the game." They wouldn't let me play chess with them. I was too impatient.

Dimandead always tried for a man's weak point. Ernie's weak point was that he had to eat. He was too self-sufficient to be lonely by himself at Dimandead and if he knew people called him "the mad hermit" it amused him. He was the most sociable of men. And he liked to smoke. Once he walked all the way from Dimandead, because the weather was too wicked to bring the horse out, and found that the storekeeper had sold his tobacco ration, thinking he wouldn't be able to get in. Ernie offered to fight him. For once he accepted cigarettes from me. The shopkeeper said he thought no man alive would cross the plains in that downpour. Ernie simmered down after a hot meal in our kitchen. But he had a dislike of shopkeepers, probably inherited from his father, who carted stores. When he spoke about shopkeepers his usual sense of humour was not in it.

He would come in and throw off his waterproof. "What's the news, Ernie?" I would ask, rushing round the kitchen waiting for the bell to ring. A meal had to be on the table when it rang. Ernie would begin on the weather. He analysed it, discussed its ailments as a man studying an opponent would size up his chances in the next round. We did not realize, surrounded by friends, neighbours and occupations, that Ernie often stayed in bed with what he called "rheumatism". He probably had, for all his strength, the slow menace of cancer that he refused to acknowledge. Coming into town for "a bit of meat for the dogs" took him away from the threat and savagery of Dimandead. What it told him with the boom of cliffs beating his life away was that it was utterly regardless of human life.

It galled Ernie, worse than the unearthly presence of Dimandead, that the townspeople, including his relations, looked on him as a failure. He was living on pumpkin and damper so that the dogs could have meat, and he was determined, at this time, to make a success of farming at Dimandead and show them all. Once he grew a wonderful crop of strawberries in the beds he had built in careful imitation of the Macgregors. I forgot what ate the strawberries, but I know the wallabies ate the tomatoes. Another year he had great golden bananas and the flying-foxes came over in clouds and tore them off the trees. Ernie waxed very humorous over the fact that no animal except man seemed to care for pumpkins. "Always got the pumpkins to fall back on." He would accept meat I kept for the dogs, but you wouldn't dare to offer him money. I always kept food for Ernie to take away with him.

Everyone in Laurieton knew that Ernie was no farmer. He wouldn't shoot the red kangaroos but encouraged them to breed up at Dimandead. The silly coots, he remarked, were always hopping out on the plain where people would shoot them. He didn't even mind the vixen stealing a fowl. She had young cubs, Ernie knew—"probably needed it more than I did". He had a rooster, he said, that could fight off hawks, and in time he might have him trained to fight off foxes. He even felt guilty about shooting an old goanna that was stealing eggs, but probably judged it a snakelike beast. One time he couldn't stay the night with us because he had to get back to the cow. She was going to calve and was uneasy without him, galloping out to meet him when he came back, lowing after him if he went out of her sight.

In his bedroom he had trouble with the swallows. They built a nest over his bed and he had to spread newspaper on himself as he lay there. He swore the mother wouldn't go out unless he was around to look after the young ones. "Reckons I'm some kind of a baby-sitter." One year he vowed he would trick them. He was fed up with the way they imposed on him. He kept the door and window shut so they couldn't get in. But he forgot and left the window open a crack while he went into town. When he came back the nest was built. "Must have had every swallow for miles in helping them. You could hear them saying to each other, 'Faster, boys, or ole Ernie'll be back before we get it finished.'" They knew he wouldn't have the heart to break it down once it was there. He wouldn't shift his bed, but he fitted a triangular piece of three-ply in the corner over his bed for protection.

Ernie would for a time lose heart when cattle broke in

and ate his orange crop. He worked like a madman, then he would give up work and curse. There were years of drought when there was no water and years of sodden wet when nothing grew.

Ernie, for all that he was slightly built, was very strong. He could run at great speed. George-with-one-arm had died, but his son Harry still kept the farm on the Moorland road. Other sons had gone to the city and prospered as suburban business-men. Ernie rode over infrequently to see Harry and on one of these visits Harry and some neighbours were trying to rope a steer. They would throw the lasso over the beast's horns and the beast would shake it off. Ernie began to grow impatient. He was smoking his pipe and glancing at the sun.

"Hey, do you want him then?" he called.

"Of course we want him. We just can't catch him."

Ernie dived at the steer with that lightning swiftness which had made him a danger to snakes when he was a child. He caught the steer by the tail and the steer promptly leapt the fence with Ernie sailing after it.

"He'll be killed."

"No, he's all right."

The steer and Ernie crashed off through the bush and twenty minutes later they heard, "Ahoy!" through the timber.

"That's Ernie," they said.

"Well, do you still want him?" he shouted. Ernie had not lost his pipe clenched between his teeth. "Come on then," he called. "If he gets his wind he'll drag me all the way to Dimandead."

"He must be physically fit," one of the men said.

"It's the bullock that was fit," Ernie retorted. "He was doing all the pulling. I just went along."

And all the time Ernie and Dimandead struggled round by round—Dimandead to starve Ernie, and Ernie, hanging on as he had hung on to the bullock's tail.

He would visit his niece Dot when he came into town and I think Dot, too, kept something for "the dogs" and saw that Ernie had more than pumpkin and damper. The baby girl put steel "butterflies" to set his curls and murmured fretfully because they were too short. The womenfolk advised him to buy blue for his washing because it was going to be in short supply.

"Buy blue," Ernie chuckled, coming into my kitchen. "They told me to buy blue." Only the cow looked over his fence when he boiled the linen in a copper in the yard and she didn't care what colour the sheets were.

Ernie was now interested in bees. He brought us treacle tins of the dark fragrant melaleuca honey, refusing payment. Later he decided it was a shame to take the honey from the bees. They needed it themselves.

Chapter VIII

WHEN I had gone off to the city—my next book was to be about jails and criminals—the people of Laurieton were not even surprised that Peg Slocombe and Roddy still rode and swam and surfed together. Nothing we did, they felt, could surprise them any more. They even felt rather pleased at owning me when they heard I had spent a week in jail.

But it caused a tremendous sensation when we joined those who had been accustomed to say, "Of course, you haven't any children, have you? Ah well, if you'd got a family you wouldn't have time for anything else."

The baby, before its birth, was known as "the jinx", but after it was born we were careful to point out that its name, Benison, meant "a blessing". It was a nuggety baby girl with black eyes, very tiny but broad and strong. "That child," Selina Slocombe said impressively, "has been here *before*."

You would see the Rodd family out rowing with the big yellow Persian cat sitting up in the prow, its whiskers blowing, and the baby on its mother's lap, enjoying the outing. Mother and child could be met on top of the mountain with the school straggling up the cliffs in front and behind. The baby rode in a linen saddle on my hip, undoubtedly cultivating its later passion for horses. It was a merry little baby, but it refused to sleep and its father and mother were exhausted by its demands for action. It had strong, beautiful hands and could be kept quiet if you gave it a paper to tear up, but if it was bored it shouted at you indignantly.

The struggle of the Rodds to rear their offspring was as good as a serial for the town and people waited impatiently for the next instalment. Girls who had left school and were not very good at lessons had always looked forward to working at the school residence. Roddy would come over and say, "Jean is leaving. She's a good little girl. It's just that she hasn't had a decent home." After little Jean had broken any ornaments and learnt to sweep under the furniture and was becoming useful, the hotel would offer her a job. Every girl wanted to work at the hotel. So I would start again. One girl had reported that "Mrs Rodd does nothing but lie all day reading". That was when I was writing a history and studying the land laws; but after the baby came nobody saw me lying down.

We had sold our horses before the baby's arrival to a neighbour who had long desired them. Betty the mare was happy with a foal and so was Creamy. They hardly recognized me.

I now had a white Saanen goat and its kid and struggled morning and night to extract milk from that goat because the baby spat out cow's milk. The goat would wait its chance until I had the billy full of milk, then it would give a sudden twist on its halter and kick the billy over.

Roddy formed the habit of sending the baby and its mother to live in a cottage some miles up the coast where one could lie in bed and see the phosphorescent ruffles of the surf break against the beach all the miles to the lighthouse at Port Macquarie. In that way he got some sleep. But after we had been cut off by flooded roads several times I refused to go to Green Hills for what he termed "a rest". We were both exhausted by coping with the baby, and the townspeople marvelled because they never had any trouble with theirs.

I was walking round the lake one morning looking for mushrooms with the baby sleeping peacefully—it always slept peacefully if it was moving—in its linen saddle on my hip. Albert Metcalfe met me and asked, with the gentle manner all the Metcalfes had, how the baby was getting on.

"It doesn't grow and I'm worried about it," I told him. "Do you think Ernie would let me go out to Diamond Head for a few weeks? The trouble is I wouldn't go unless Ernie would let me pay him. So I don't like to ask him."

At this time we had more money than we had ever had, in spite of my paying income tax in England and another income tax in Australia. There was even a steady demand for *Lost Haven* at the local store. I would wheel the baby's pram over full of copies with the ginger cat sitting on top. Getting the author to provide autographed copies was a little perquisite of the local shop, though I got no royalty on these.

"Why wouldn't Ernie let you pay him?" Albert said indignantly. It was just one more proof what a stuck-up snob his young brother was. "He's only battling like the rest of us." He promised to have a word with Ernie, and Roddy had a word with him, too. So Ernie came in in the sulky to take me and the·baby to Dimandead. The baby shouted approvingly when she saw the horse as though she knew what it was. The ginger cat came. If anyone regarded our going as improper Ernie was likely to pay as much attention as I did.

Ernie had papered the little room off the veranda with clean newspaper. The baby played naked in the beach ripples and grew fat and strong. She slept under the shadow of the trees where now the rutile mine has gouged out an eroded quarry to pave its roads. She slept all night in the little room papered with newspaper.

Roddy came out in the town taxi at the week-end with rare foods to find a brown and jolly little baby. After that you couldn't keep us away from Dimandead. Terry Ewen, the taxi-owner, was eloquent about the track. "I tell you, my boy, a man must be hard up for a crust to drive over it. Stumps, corrugations, pot-holes, streams clear *and* muddy —the lot! It has them all. Nothing that the human mind can conceive is missing from that goddam road." Terry only took us there out of friendship. It humiliated him to be bogged to the axles in liquid mud and to see Ernie come jogging to the rescue, standing up in the cart like a charioteer, with a shovel and two six-foot lengths of board to put under the wheels.

To save Terry's taxi from breaking up altogether I bought the fish-truck from Len Shoesmith. It was so high off the ground it could pass right over stumps. The men of the town could not understand why I drove the truck. Roddy never wished to do so. He learnt to drive some years later when our son arrived. It lowered a man's pride, men who wanted to borrow my truck thought, to have to ask a woman. Whenever their own trucks broke down they came to ask the loan of the Erskine, knowing I wouldn't refuse a milkman or baker who had to get through flooded roads.

We would pack the cat, Didger, and the baby and the baby's gear and the swimming costumes and food, the chessboard and the typewriter, in the truck and if we bogged in sight of Dimandead it was a case of, "Go for Ernie".

Ernie always pretended to be exasperated at the stupidity of truck- and car-owners. "I knew how it would be," he would begin, leaping out of the cart and seizing his shovel. "People enjoy getting bogged just so's I can dig them out. They make a habit of it. Do it on purpose. The other night I hear a car revving out on the plain and I'm ijjut enough to take a hurricane lamp and go to see what's up. Two women—" he waved his eyebrows like a distracted moth—"two women in one of these undersized cars like the runt of the litter. Now why would they be wanting to cross the plains in the *dark*? Took me an hour and a half to dig them out. Next time I hear someone mucking about miles from anywhere I'm going to go to bed in a hurry and put the light out." But he wouldn't have.

Sometimes I tried to be clever and cut a new track avoiding the bogholes of the "beach road". "I might have known it," Ernie would lament. "I wouldn't even take the *horse* through there."

Ernie swore that if there was ever a real "made" road to Dimandead he would buy himself a motor-scooter. He was seventy-five before he bought the motor-scooter and the road was loose gravel and dangerous, but he rode it just the same.

We loved Ernie and Dimandead equally, but we knew we rather overflowed his house. Even Didger would stretch out on the hearth among the dogs, monopolizing the fire.

"I know," I said, struck by an inspiration when we were

all getting in each other's way in Ernie's kitchen. "How would it be if Ernie sold us a piece of land he didn't want and we put up a shack on it? Then when we came out Ernie would still have this place to himself."

Roddy looked inquiringly at Ernie, who narrowed his eyes as he did when he was thinking.

"I know just the place," he said. "Over by the creek. Remember when you rode through with Len Shoesmith that time, and I showed you the short cut? I've always thought I'd like to build a house there. It's sheltered from the wind and it gets the sun."

We all set off across the paddocks to look at it, the baby riding on Ernie's shoulder and the cat and dogs bounding ahead. The corner paddock sloped down to the stream that ran from what had once been the lake and was now a mere pond. Around it was a growth of huge and beautiful paperbarks and she-oaks. Ernie mentioned later that the first Pullen house had stood here, and we found in the thick scrub higher on the slope four stumps that had once held up the house. But there was no other trace. Dimandead had covered and obliterated them all. The great white paperbarks were in flower, sending down a shower of pale stamens on Ernie's beard as he looked up to see his bees at work. The heavy honey-scent had attracted flutterings of white butterflies. At least they seemed white, but their underwings were gold and scarlet and blue and black. Small yellow beetles tumbled in the flowers. Benison found a low curved bough and adopted it as her "horse tree" for riding.

"If you don't let us pay for it the deal's off," I told Ernie.

"Right. It'll cost you five pounds."

I told him he was out of his mind. We would have a surveyor come out and measure the paddock and say what was a fair price. The surveyor had some difficulty getting there in his jeep, but he and his assistant drove in white pegs where they were promptly lost in the undergrowth and said the land was worth sixty-five pounds. So I went to the office of the solicitor who visited Laurieton once a week and instructed him to draw up the necessary documents. When Ernie came into town to change his books he was dumbfounded. "It's far too much," he insisted. He walked over to the solicitor and ordered him to make the price five pounds. This went on for some weeks, with me holding out for sixty-five pounds and Ernie insisting on five. "I'm selling the land and I've got a right to say what I'm selling it for."

"And I'm buying the land and I've got a right to say what I'm paying."

This haggling went on until the solicitor refused to take my instructions and I sacked him. Ernie promptly came in great triumph to say he'd hired him. "Seeing he's mine he'll have to do what I tell him." The land was sold for sixty-five pounds.

Ernie was still incredulous about the price. The respect the town now showed him as a landowner who was very smart in a deal was a little quenched when someone broke into his house to search for the money. Ernie had to lock his door when he came into town and it made him uneasy.

Roddy, who took great pleasure in planning and directing, took advantage of Ernie's new status as a man of wealth. Ernie decided to build the house himself and we refused to let him unless he was paid to do so. We bought the gyprock and timber for the flooring, and my father, with great craft, for building materials were still on some kind of wartime ration, procured me some second-grade iron roofing. The great mahogany slabs, two inches thick, which formed the outer walls Ernie brought from the old barn.

He began to chop down the tall paperbarks and dynamite out those that resisted. As a miner he loved dynamite. He had a bushman's fear of trees about a house. Every time he cut down a tree there was a dramatic scene with myself as prima donna and Roddy and the baby as appreciative audience. Ernie took no notice. He went on clearing.

The first summer, as though Dimandead had made a sudden bid against this new invasion, a fire leapt the creek and came so close to the house that one window cracked in the heat. Ernie fought the fire single-handed and when we arrived he was standing sooty with ash in his beard in a blackened desert with the house safe in the middle.

After that he would "burn off" every winter whether I liked it or not. There was one gaunt ring-barked tree which the birds used as a look-out post. Benison would watch them through binoculars. We came back one holiday and the tree was gone.

"Ernie, you old devil," I yelled, "you've cut down the *tree*!"

"Fifteen years," Ernie began, "she's been on to me about that tree. What an eyesore it was standing there ring-barked. And now it isn't there and she's still not satisfied." He had these sudden impulses to improve our corner while we were away. He would fence it. One year he put up a small lavatory but never got as far as the roof.

Ernie never ceased to take pleasure in the shack. This took the form of lamenting how he had always meant to build himself a house there. Along *we* came and put up a house in the *very* place—cool in summer, warm in winter, protected from the westerlies and southerlies, which you couldn't say for that house of Clara's. "You don't need to sweep *that*. All you have to do is open the door and the wind blows the dirt straight out the back. Open the door when the wind changes and it blows it straight out the front." This chant of Ernie's always concluded with his knocking out his pipe and looking up the chimney to remark how well it was drawing. What he was saying was: "I have given my friends a priceless gift and we are enjoying it together."

The chimney was his masterpiece, constructed of great rocks which he hoisted up and cemented into place. When I wailed that we should never have let Ernie build the house, it would kill him, Roddy replied, "He's enjoying himself. Concentrate on being sorry for me."

Roddy was the unskilled labour going out at week-ends to hold up the ceiling or walls while Ernie hammered them into place. Not since Ernie drained the lake had he tackled anything that turned out such a great success. The system of Macgregor-gardens would have been equally successful had it not been for the birds and animals. The Rodd house, which was still standing when Benison and her brother were grown up, had two windows in the solid mahogany walls and a veranda later extended to provide extra sleeping space. We cooked over the open fire.

While the house was going up Roddy would walk the seven miles from Laurieton on Friday evening, leaving me to cope with visitors and odd jobs. He would be holding up the ceiling like Atlas while Ernie hammered the nails. Then he would go surfing or they would declare a chess tournament or just sit in the sun. Once the rain was so heavy Ernie had to ferry Roddy back across the plains in the sulky, the dogs swimming in front, each in its separate ripple. Fine weather Roddy would go along the beach, surfing every now and then. We never knew if we would see him again because once, looking down on his favourite surfing place from the cliffs, he saw five sharks lying on the bottom of the clear water. It was a hot day and he was so indignant that he just waited till they began to move before he went in.

The legend in Laurieton had been that Ernie was a shiftless hermit. Ernie performed miracles of toil. After the house was built he would say quietly that he was going to do "a bit of fencing up along the cliffs where old Baldy fell over". This fencing included felling the trees, splitting them into fence-posts, digging holes, boring through the posts, straining the wires. The unfortunate Baldy was a carcass hanging in a tree at the foot of the cliff when we first came and the white skeleton little by little dropped to pieces until only the skull with curved horns remained. Finally all of Baldy was gone. Gradually the earth of Dimandead claimed whatever the sea did not wash away. One year all the sand had gone from the beach leaving black rock. "It'll all be back," Ernie prophesied, and next year this was so.

The lagoon would be six feet deep. Then the following year it would be up to your ankles. But year by year the little plume of smoke would go up from the chimney Ernie built. Ernie would arrive for dinner and the chessboard and the demijohn of wine would be brought out. He would bring a pumpkin or a cabbage to add to the feast and draw up his chair with great appetite to my cooking. "Nothing like a stew. It curves round your ribs." Or, "What I like is an underdone potato. Always like my potatoes with bones in them."

Ernie believed in the philosophy of ascetic excess. "I like

a good gorge," he said. "Take the blackfeller now. He only eats one sort of thing at a time. Once you've eaten enough lobsters you don't want any more. The thing is to have *enough*. The blackfeller would eat fish until he didn't want to see a fish again. Then he'd go inland and eat bunya-bunya nuts or remember the wild plums were ripe. When he'd had enough of those he'd go off and eat something else. That's the way we ought to be. None of this business of eating a lot of different things at once."

Almost before Benison could walk he had her on the back of Princess and would stride beside her holding her on. He would be off with her to show her some nest or haunt of animals. There were hares that came out at dusk in the dew. There were koala trees that only they knew of. Ernie claimed that if you wanted to study rare animals you ought to watch what the cats brought in. He had them trained to bring him anything they caught and bring it alive. Then he rewarded them. There was one cat on whose collecting instincts Ernie expanded. He told of the rare little creatures the cat found and brought to lay at his feet. "Little fellers I'd never come across myself. But the old cat found them. She'd sit and look at me when she brought them the way a mother cat looks when it brings its kitten a mouse. Never hurt them. Just picked them up in her mouth and brought them to me." We were sceptical of Ernie's collector cat. We did not like to say that it probably only brought him what it couldn't eat itself. An occasional rare phalanger bestowed on Ernie was probably just dessert which the cat did not feel it wanted after a hearty meal, but Ernie would not believe this.

By the time Benison was in her teens and an art student she was also a Nature bore. "What," she would demand of some young man, "are you doing to protect the kangaroos in Queensland?" And without our noticing it Benison grew up in Ernie's philosophy, which was suitable to an Australian bushman of the nineteenth century. God for Benison wore a grey flannel undershirt and looked on any kind of complaining or self-pity as unworthy, unless it was humorous and a ripple on the top of conversation. He valued patience and quiet.

"Now why do you have to be rushing about?" Ernie would demand of me. "Look at Roddy, look at me lying in the sun. When you're with experts like us who know how to laze you ought to profit by our example."

His generosity was not civilized. It was that of a native tribesman. He explained this by saying that he hadn't got anything valuable. "It's only when a man gets to owning a heap of stuff that he starts saying, 'Hands off!'"

There was one person who, knowing this reckless generosity of Ernie's, suffered agonies of worry over the sale of the acres by the creek. This was Bert Bullen, Clara's son, referred to by Ernie as "the nephew". Because he had broken his arm at Dimandead he never passed exams, but became head waiter at the Journalists' Club, which is a fine place to pick up tips on the stock exchange. Bert was saving to retire so that he could join Uncle at Dimandead. The place worked on him even at a distance. It was his mirage, beautiful and enticing. Bert now wrote desperately begging Uncle not to sell any more land. He had a picture of Dimandead flenched into building lots, each with a square box of house on it. If Uncle wanted money he only had to ask. That was what Ernie would never do. He would fend for himself even if he starved.

Besides, he was rich now. He wrote consolingly to Bert promising he would not sell any more land. Bert could not come to Dimandead then, but he realized that the Metcalfe reverence for property was somewhere deep down. Ernie would not dissipate Bert's inheritance and squander it on high living. Sometimes now when he came into town he would go down to the hotel and engage in convivial exchange. He still lived mostly on bread, corned beef and pumpkin. But his reputation as a mad hermit was on the wane, though it did not entirely vanish. Two visitors called in and told us how they had been lost crossing the plain.

"And then we came to this gate and went through it, with enormous trees and bushes everywhere, until we came out and saw a house in the distance. So we drove up and a pack of savage dogs came barking out at us. And then a piece of sacking was drawn away from a broken window and a terrible bearded face peered out. I tell you we got away from there—fast!"

We tried to explain that the dogs had come out, Pup and Bluey and Ole Mammy, barking welcome and Ernie was the terrible bearded face. He was looking out to see if it was us. "That was our friend." They were not impressed.

Chapter IX

Ernie had been much taken with the white Saanen goats, which multiplied and bred and now that Benison no longer would drink their milk were purely decorative. The kids sported up and down the fallen pine trunk donated by Uncle Johnny. They would tiptoe into the house by night led by their mother and leap on the table to eat fruit, smashing the bowl as they did so. We would wake up and see the great billygoat standing with his front feet on the mantelpiece while he cropped off a vase of azaleas. You could not leave a door open for them, but they were elegant creatures.

One early morning I came into the bush-house and the queen of the herd was stretched out giving birth. This time she had twins, snowy and immaculate, complete with hoofs and hair, wrapped in a shining transparent envelope. Within an hour they were teetering about on their high-heeled little hoofs. To see these young goats born was almost to be converted to Ernie's philosophy of Nature, which at other times I regarded as too trusting and optimistic. He was assured that there was nothing this mysterious force he called Nature would not in time make perfect. He altogether overlooked the sinister side of the life force.

"In a thousand years," Ernie would say, waving the thousand years away with his hand, "Nature will have fixed it all up again." This Nature of his was like The Mother, it was his divine Sapphira, a feminine force caring for the young, always working and planning and bringing into being. Time for Ernie was infinite. He told us how once he was lying looking at the stars so intently that he felt himself lifted from the earth. I regarded time as something I snatched minute by minute. Ernie and Dimandead might have thousands of years between them, but I had none to waste, was always hasty and distracted. I envied them.

Ernie, hearing me lamenting over damage by the goats, offered to buy them. I gave them to him gladly.

"I've always liked goats," he said, accepting them. "But these big white ones are a cut above the little fellers round here."

I had promised the animal husbandry expert who sent them to keep the strain pure and mentioned this to Ernie. I might have known he would have a theory. He jutted his beard stubbornly when he heard about keeping the strain pure.

"Now that is not the way Nature works," he contended. "Stands to reason that the more you cross animals the more likely you are to come up with something new. Don't matter if it takes a thousand years or so . . ."

"Yes, but Ernie . . ."

He also had a theory that weeds were good for the soil and should not be removed from between the "furrers". They kept the soil moist and prevented evaporation. He scorned those farmers who found their soil all dried out because they removed weeds that were doing a good job, sheltering the young plants. He had another theory that it was not wearing clothes that wore them out, but washing them. "Women always at them, wash, wash, wash. What happens? The clothes fall to pieces."

So it was no surprise when I heard he had bought the Twomey goats when Old Pop retired from Humbug. Ernie brought them over to cross with mine. The white goats refused to associate with the brown and brindle goats and drove them up on to the cliffs where they foraged happily. Ernie liked to look out on the white herd sporting on the green behind his house. He taught the big billygoat to wrestle with him and at sight of him it would rear up on its hind legs, inviting him to fight. The herd followed him over to our shack and took possession of a heap of gravel left from the house building where they butted each other off. They stood on their hind legs, bending down and breaking every scrub, delicately nibbling the tips, and in no time at all had eaten off every wattle in the paddocks.

When we went down to the beach to look for driftwood they followed along, with the cow bobbing anxiously among them, not letting Ernie out of her sight. He never bought timber when building our house if he could find what suited him on the beach and would shoulder baulks of timber that Roddy and I together could not have lifted. Most of the softwood in our house floated ashore, washed up among fishermen's glass floats, weed, bluebottles, nautilus and uprooted mangroves.

This amity with the herd of goats might have continued had not the billygoat developed a vicious streak and challenged me to fight as I was crossing the paddock, rearing up and striking at me with its sharp hooves. I sent it scampering, but I was worried lest it knock Benison over, for it was bigger than she was. I persuaded Ernie to drive the billygoat away on to the cliffs, and at first the goat was hurt by the treachery of its friend. But Ernie, who secretly hoped for a goat-cross with the brindled herd, persisted in shooing him away. The goat took the hint and removed his white herd to the cliffs where they found the salty herbs and acrid shoots so to their liking that they made only periodic visits to the homestead.

This was the prelude to a tragedy. Ernie had always allowed fishermen to drive through his fences and up on the cliffs with their cars or trucks. While he was in town a gang of them came out and shot all the goats, the brindle-brown and the white Saanens, loading what they wanted for meat on the trucks, skinning what they did not want for the hides, and throwing the bodies down a crevice. Some were killed as they leapt down the rocks and Ernie, wondering why the goats did not come home, found their bodies. Only old Billy and one son escaped. The old billygoat was far too cunning to be shot.

When Ernie came next into town even his hair seemed to have turned red with anger. He sat down on the wooden bench in the kitchen and related how he had tracked the men across the plains and up the Moorland road until he lost the tracks in a criss-cross of other tyres. I advised he should go to the police. "If I can't track them the police can't," he said. "I've got a pretty fair idea who done it." He waited for the men to come with his rifle always handy. But why should they come back? They had made a clean sweep.

Because not one doe escaped the slaughter Dimandead was spared the erosion of ancient Greece. About fifteen years later I heard Ernie remarking with approval that the wattles were coming back again and that Nature was wonderful. He liked to see the cattle enjoying the shade of the wattles. "A dry camp for them and good shelter."

I had felt some remorse at having prompted him to banish Ole Billy, but Ernie was too fair-minded to think it was my fault. However, the disaster affected some deep spring of trust in him. He had always been free and friendly with chance comers. Now the latent landed-proprietor, inherited perhaps from his Welsh ancestors, was aroused. He put up a "No Trespassers" sign by the gate. He repaired the fences, running wires across the tracks the fishermen had been accustomed to use.

The track, no longer brushed by wheels, was soon deep in flowering bushes. The crossing over the creek running down from the cliff became impassable. More of Dimandead reverted to wild growth, fewer people came there. When Ernie found some young men shooting on his land he went out with his rifle and "frightened hell out of them", deliberately exploiting his mad hermit reputation to keep people away.

But about this time he made another friend. Alan Mobbs, who had a small farm on the Moorland road, had once seen Ernie when he was a young boy and asked Harry Metcalfe, "Who's that old bloke?" "That's my Uncle Ernie, lives at Dimandead." Twelve years later Alan Mobbs met Ernie again out on the plains. He had been herding a mob of bullocks and his horse had galloped off and left him so he was walking. Ernie helped him round up the cattle. Later Alan rode to Dimandead and, as the place always did, it held what a man desired most. For Alan it was feed for his cattle, a dream of Paradise green and deep when his own paddocks were parched and bare.

Twelve months later he was bogged on the plains in his truck and Ernie dug him out.

They became friends and Alan struck an agistment rate with Ernie on a yearly basis for so many head of cattle. He would leave his farm at daylight, drove the mob down and get a feed.

"I wouldn't say he was a clean washer-up," said Alan. "He'd put the plates on the floor for the pups and cats. Said it took the rough off them."

"Always go easy on water," Ernie advised Alan. In the old days in Queensland, he told him, he reckoned he could last two days over a dry stretch on two billycans of water. Half a billycan was for a drink. The other half was for cooking and to boil for tea. On foot you could carry two billycans with you and get through at least a day, a night and the next day. When you were prospecting you sometimes couldn't take a horse. It needed too much water.

Alan observed that the white ants had eaten through the floor under Ernie's stove which, as he said, "sank and reposed on Mother earth". Ernie threw out the stove in the back yard and hatched ducklings in the place it had occupied. He reckoned the foxes wouldn't get them there. He rigged a stick across two uprights in the back yard to boil the billy.

The old cat had a litter of kittens in the sideboard in the kitchen whose walls and ceiling had sooted up to a fine Rembrandt brown. So that the mother cat could get to her young when he was away Ernie had knocked out a pane of glass from the window and covered this with a sack. In the wet, frogs used to flop through the opening to hunt flies in the lamplight and the rain came in with them. Kittens popped through the hole in the floor and as Roddy and Ernie played chess with Ernie's old cardboard men the mother cat would pounce on the table and sweep them aside with her tail. Clara's house was reverting to the wild.

Ernie's hens came in and pecked for crumbs by day, and they so liked to roost on the cane settee on the back veranda that he finally put it down in the fowl-pen. "Reckon they get more use out of it than I do."

About this time Ernie and Dimandead seemed to have come to some equilibrium. With the cattle providing him with a small income Ernie no longer tried to make a living from agriculture. He still tended his bees and kept his ditches clear. He "burnt off", keeping down undergrowth. The paddocks were now green parks and glades with the red-and-white cattle cropping them.

The mysterious "rheumatism" which had been painful for so long vanished completely. For many years thereafter he was strong and well. Dimandead and Ernie, an irresistible force meeting an immovable obstacle, were to remain in adjustment. Perhaps Dimandead had accepted him, even then, as part of itself, a protector rather than a nuisance.

Chapter X

THERE WERE PEOPLE who somehow did not find that Dimandead brought out the best in them. Benison's godmother, Doris, had been with me on some very rough trips and had once suffered heroically and silently for days when she tripped over an iron tent-peg. But she was not silent about Dimandead. Benison and I had taken her out especially to see it and we were bogged. I set off at a run to bring Ernie. Doris and Benison, becoming impatient, took a short cut that Benison knew over some rough country while Ernie and I were coming back by road.

Doris's description of how they were met by a pack of huge and savage dogs was only a prelude to how she sat in a sooty kitchen with rain beating through a broken pane covered by sacking. The cats spat at the dogs and the dogs growled at the cats and kittens popped up through a hole in the floor. I had snatched Ernie from his washing-up, and dirty dish-water mixed with toast crusts made pools on the kitchen table.

When Ernie and I arrived he brewed tea hospitably and, as a mark of honour, took out a cream cake which had been kept in a tin for a special occasion. In the dark kitchen he did not notice that the cream had gone green. I told Doris afterwards that she had only to make some excuse and scrape off the cream on the back veranda as I did, but she seemed to brood on it. She was an editor and whenever I saw her in her city office she would say, "What about the man with the beard? Is he still living in that awful place?"

But the Rodds always looked forward to doing their accustomed rounds and our spirits lifted when Dimandead lay before us. Ernie's house was not to be seen from ours nor was our house in Ernie's line of sight. Two paddocks, a belt of trees and the rise of the ground lay between. We would drive up by the lake and round by Ernie's back door to leave the magazines and papers. Ernie would be standing under the grape trellis or he would come to the door. The truck would then jounce off over the open paddock where Jack's "furrers" were fast sinking into the turf, carefully through the gutter of stream. The she-oaks brushed us as we came through the clearing.

Ernie found me constructing a causeway over the little run of water that joined his creek so that we were bounded by water on two sides of our land. Taking the stones from me, he fitted them together so expertly that they never washed away. Before the visitors and food were unpacked he would be striding across with a cabbage or pumpkin under his arm.

There came at different times a racing driver, the pretty Viennese who managed a dress shop, a great scholar and university librarian, a crocodile hunter from the Northern Territory, a swimming champion and his manager, all kinds of people. I would put on the dinner and follow the others to the beach or Ernie and Roddy would settle to games of chess on the side veranda or in front of the fire.

We would go down by the creek, round the south flank of the hill to the lagoon on the beach, walking along towards the cliffs to find pipis for bait or going down the immense emptiness towards Crowdy Head to see if some far object in the blowing mist was worth our beachcombing. Usually it was only a tree-trunk washed ashore, but we would find hatch-covers from ships, timber, purple nautilus shells, and once a small bench which was added to the house furniture.

I might leave Roddy surfing, Benison and Ernie catching the horse, and go up around the cliffs to the "diamond mine", with a knapsack on my back and a knife to scrape out the quartz crystals. A German firm had mined there for industrial diamonds before World War I, but now there were only three low mounds of upturned clay overgrown with prickly hakea. Sometimes picnic parties from Laurieton fossicked there, digging out what looked like pendants from a lost chandelier and mislaying them after they reached home.

Behind Ernie's house was the disused trail up to the cliffs, along them to the trig station on the highest ridge above the diamond mine. Only once did I strike home in a direct line and was lost in a maze of thickly timbered gullies, the undergrowth higher than my head. Benison was very scornful. A green tree-snake six feet long jumped straight up on its tail, a beautiful creature whipping away in panic. When I regained the cliffs the sunset showed me two great golden beasts from a myth, curved horns, shining manes. They were the two survivor goats leaping for their caves when they scented me.

All to the west spread the coloured plains, swamps,

moors, the Comboyne faded by distance to dim blue behind the dark trio of peaks, the Three Brothers.

Once Ernie and I took a German refugee, Gundel, up to the diamond mine, and as we paused on the cliffs under a wrinkled banksia tree Gundel looked at the empty country with such depression and longing. "So much land," he said. He had spent years in a refugee camp in Spain after his escape from Hitler's Germany. His eyes devoured the beauty and openness with a terrible craving. The atmosphere about him grew black with his sadness as he thought of the old countries like a worn doorstep trodden by the feet of centuries and the thousands who would have flung themselves on such country, hordes of human locusts.

Ernie stood looking attentively at Gundel from under the brim of his army hat. He wondered that the sight did not make Gundel free and joyful. To me, who did not ever want possessions because I had always been lucky and careless enough to throw them behind me and walk on, there was something horrible in the craving to own all that your eye fell on. But I had never endured the wretchedness of a refugee camp or been hungry for just a little more bread. The slums had been beautiful behind St Mary's Cathedral with the great oaks in the park coming into leaf and the bells chiming at night. There had been the uncanny mountains of the Warrumbungles, the mid-west with its contented towers of grain. But poor Gundel, who taught me to cook a dish of fried rice with a few vegetables and a little pork cut small, a dish that would stretch to any number of people, brought his misery with him and settled in the ugliest and dreariest of Sydney's outer suburbs.

After some years he decided to return to Spain with his

wife and daughter. Better to be very poor in the Balearic Islands, he said, than endure the ugly living places of Australians. The poorest peasants in Europe had more fun. And at their farewell in a city garret there were guitars and wine, men with gold rings in their ears, yells of "*Olé!*" and Spanish dancing. Gundel claimed that if he stayed in Australia for ever he would never own the land he wanted.

Ernie and the Rodds had different views about owning land. The Rodds believed that nobody should be allowed to own land outright, but only be able to lease it for a lifetime. The administration of the land should be the supreme work of any government, and those who did not enrich their land should not be left to ruin it. Ernie claimed that a feller wasn't going to do much to a property unless he owned it lock, stock and barrel. Maybe he might cut down all the trees like we said and leave it an eroded bit of dirt, but these days (Ernie seized an illogical point) Science could do wonderful things. Nature would restore the worst desert if men didn't get in the way. We didn't believe him and said so. He didn't really believe it himself.

"A thousand years . . ." he murmured.

"A thousand years and it'd still be ruined. Show me a desert and I'll show you where there were once thousands of people who ruined the land."

Ernie and I were down by the lagoon one morning and I was examining the sparkling grains in the clear water. "That is gold, Ernie," I said.

Ernie, who had prospected all over the continent, stroked his beard. "Alluvial," he said. "Only a trace. You'd need heavy expensive equipment to get it."

"And that black stuff," I pointed to the outline of dark mineral round the ripples, "is probably valuable, too. The beach is coated with it. If we staked a claim and put up a notice it would prevent other people coming to dig up the creek."

On the other side of Laurieton along the beach when we first came some local men had a claim in the grey soil behind the sand-dunes but gave up because there was not enough gold.

Ernie looked at me with the same clear, considering inquiry that he had turned on Gundel. I felt mean. To him, the idea of staking a claim to prevent anyone else from doing so was abhorrent. If you couldn't or didn't want to mine yourself, why prevent anyone else mining?

I had a strong foreboding about this, and sure enough I came down to the beach a year later to find a sharp stake driven into the ground with the notice of a mining claim. I made a great outcry about it.

"I told you, I told you, this would happen."

Ernie only stroked his beard. "Some silly cove with more hope than sense," he said. "Just on spec he puts this up. Maybe never do anything about it."

The notice faded. The post slanted and presently became part of the landscape.

Ernie had strong opinions as an old miner about landlords too mean to let you cross their land to look for ore. "Some of them'd shoot you sooner."

We both felt without saying so that Dimandead was a state of mind. People came there worn down with worries and after a few days of that enveloping silence and peace, with the birds singing in the clearing and the creek pouring into the deep brown pool where we washed off the salt from surfing on our way back up the leafy track, their anxieties were smoothed out, they lived minute by minute in the sunlight, fleeting the time carelessly as they did in the golden world. But others were too far gone in civilization; the silence made them uneasy and they hurried away, casting glances of dread over their shoulder at the roaring bulk of cliffs and sea which might swallow up their little day.

It depended on your own disposition how Dimandead affected you, and only Ernie could live there permanently because he had grown close to the hidden and awful character of Dimandead, an old bushman solitary but never lonely.

Ernie was supposed to be some kind of philosophical anarchist. I never found out what his real politics were, although they were of a ferocious and leftist nature. Actually he was just Australian democratic, certain that he held life and fate in his own scarred and resolute hands. We spent many pleasant hours denouncing not only our own country's government but that of every other country. If they had only followed his advice years ago, Ernie would say, his eyes merry, when he was first ready to give it to them, the Government could have made a much better fist of everything they'd done. Because, he said, the essence of democracy is that fellers who know nothing about what they're advising the Government on, such as himself, couldn't do much worse than all the experts had.

With or without Ernie's advice the country was changing and even little Laurieton was losing all its old lawless character. Old Sam the puntman had been only too pleased to let us row passengers over in his leaky boat while we admired the sunset. Now we had a new, efficient and smiling Dutchman with a new engine-driven punt.

We had intended to stay in Laurieton two years, long enough to write my novel. We were there eleven. Towards the end Head Office would recollect that they had a graduate secondary-school teacher in a fishing village and would offer Roddy charge of some intermediate high school. He would enlist Terry Ewen and his taxi and drive across half the State over the week-end. I would be waiting impatiently with Benison for their return and would hear the taxi draw up in the dark and Roddy laughing at the last of Terry's jokes as the door slammed.

"What was the school like?" I would demand, bringing food.

"Terrible. Poor devil ended up by wanting to swap me. He was on the edge of a nervous breakdown. All the edges were white and I think the pansies in the school garden had their faces washed separately each morning. And wealthy! That school had all the latest gadgets—his Parents and Citizens were running him into the ground."

He would send a telegram declining promotion once again, and I would be downcast that by marrying him I had ruined his career. When two inspectors made a special visit to the school they had to step over the tame wallaby, which was lying on the path with the cat between its paws. The wallaby refused to move.

The cat and the wallaby were great friends, touching noses whenever they met. But there came the terrible day when a stream of children, in great distress, could be seen coming in the gate bearing on a bier the body of the lion cat. It was given a ceremonial interment at the end of the garden. The children of Laurieton had a feeling for funerals because, by old custom, when anyone in the town died the school flag flew at half-mast and they were all drawn up in ranks in the playground as the cortège went past. To have omitted this custom would have given great offence.

It was the cat's duty, which it had chosen for itself, to purr Benison to sleep in the evening, and the night after its burial the great purring was heard as usual. The baby stretched out her hand to the lordly presence, for the cat had not yet realized it was dead and it took its accustomed place at the side of her bed. The next night it did not come.

Benison was now old enough to make a pest of herself trying to join the other children in school, being ejected by the staff. There were four assistants and the school appeared to be swelling like yeast. There were swings and seesaws and a great deal of climbing equipment in the playground. Benison, when thrust out of the school, would console herself by taking to a high horizontal ladder, swinging from one metal rung through the air to grasp another. "I can't bear to look," her grandfather said, covering his face. When Benison was at high school years later the only report I can remember said: "Benison is a magnificent little athlete and gymnast." She was so tiny that we paved the way of specialists with gold, but they only told us that some combination of genes accounted for her size. Her father came of the small swarthy Cornish people who mined tin and, earlier, lived in caves in the ground and were feared by the large blond in-comers. Benison had the Cornish build, their stature, their intimacy with the earth. As an art student she brought earth and pebbles from Diamond Head and experimented with clay and ochre for her pictures. She had no liking for books, only for animals.

I would telephone our doctor when Benison could crawl to say that she had just had another fall from a high place, and the doctor would comment unfeelingly, "Lucky she fell on her head", while Benison would smile merrily. Later, when she had a horse, she would stagger into the shack at Diamond Head and report she had landed on soft earth and I needn't make all that fuss. She had Ernie's habit of making light of hurts.

We now had a doctor in Laurieton, Ella Brunswick, an Irishwoman with four children, two at the school. She had had many adventures during the war and when it ended went searching for her husband, an Austrian and a prisoner of the Russian army. The Brunswicks built a fine house, with a surgery for Ella, next to the church. Rudl, her husband, played the cello and ran the local newspaper. Ella was not only an intelligent and reliable doctor, she was brave. She would go out at midnight to leave her car at the foot of some mountain in the Comboyne and be pulled up the steeps on a horse-drawn milk sledge, sturdily grasping her doctor's bag. She would cross flooded creeks, go over terrible tracks, to reach a patient.

Rudl Brunswick offended the returned soldiers by telling them that when their planes came over Hamburg he was on the anti-aircraft gun waiting to shoot them down. He had joined the Nazis when they entered Vienna because, like many young Austrians, he had felt they were offering something better than Schuschnigg's rule. We begged Rudl to be more tactful with the Laurieton people, but, with his sweet smile, in his rich tenor voice he said just what he pleased.

The handsome Rudl was once taken aback. He was holding forth in front of our fire about the laziness of Australians, their reluctance to work. "What would do them all good," he said, smiling, "would be a little *pushed* labour. Not forced labour—no, no—but pushed."

Roddy asked, "And they would be all organized in gangs?"

"Yes." Rudl considered. "Possibly for roads and other works."

"There's only one thing that would ruin your scheme." Roddy's voice was as pleasant as Rudl's.

"And what is that?" Rudl asked.

"Well, you would be in charge of a gang, Rudl, and if it ever got to that stage, I would be in one of the gangs. And when your back was turned, Rudl, I would smash in your head with a shovel."

Rudl explained that he was only *theoretically* ready to form work gangs and Roddy said he was only theoretically going to smash in Rudl's head with a shovel. After that Rudl did not so often criticize Australians. Twenty years later you could not tell Rudl, a distinguished public servant in Canberra, from any other Australian except by his extreme neatness and efficiency. He and quiet, sturdy Ella put their four children through the university—and how they worked!

I was writing a book about travelling bee-keepers, *The Honey Flow*, and Jack Koina, the boss of a bee-keeping outfit, came on a visit. When Rudl kissed my hand as he appeared for an evening of music Jack never flickered an eyelash, but later, hundreds of miles away, for the benefit of his friends round the campfire, he would give an imitation of Rudl telling about his courtship of Ella when she was a young doctor and he a ski instructor in the Austrian Alps. "I see zese girls," Jack mimicked, "and I say, 'I will have the one with the pretty ankles and the big income.'" Rudl worshipped Ella, tended her when she was tired in a way that would have amazed our fishermen, who thought their wives best occupied waiting on them.

The new people at the post office had also this middle-class view that a husband and wife were a working team of equals. Mac was our new postmaster and he and his wife Bonte came from the New England ranges where I was now going off to work with the bee-keepers. Bonte's mother, who was nicknamed James, supervised holiday cottages on the North Haven side of the breakwater. James had more loving-kindness than any woman I have known. She had had great tragedies, but had flowed over them as a wave sweeps over a rock.

Bonte, who was pretty and elegant, liked social occasions, influential and exciting people, and musical evenings. She drove her two sons twenty-five miles so they could have violin lessons. The music club met at the school residence and Roddy bought an imposing new radiogram so that we could all listen to the records of classical music. The Brunswicks, the McLachlans, the Rodds, would gather round our fire and the great symphonies would be booming out, and then there would be the voice of Bonte, "Stop! Could we just have Coda A again? I missed the entrance of the clarinets."

My interest in symphonies was tepid. My mother, who now came to rule the school residence when I was on my travels, played the pipe organ and my childhood had had a background of Bach. I never became a competent musician because practice interfered with basketball and we always had mother to play for us when we sang innocently round the piano. Everyone sang in our house when I was young.

Secretly I thought it rather pretentious to study the nine Beethoven symphonies, and down in the Pilliga scrub, arriving in camp dirty and sweaty, I would give a glad cry, "It's Tuesday and I've missed another symphony!" My bee-keepers thought "You Are My Honeysuckle" was the height of music. They sang as they pushed the big trucks over the back roads through the forest. "Go for Ernie!" they would yell when they were bogged.

Bonte and James always brought the supper for the musical gatherings, Bonte remarking that if they left it to me they would find themselves eating dry biscuits with a hunk of cheese on top.

"And you want cream cakes?"

"Certainly I want cream cakes." Bonte smiled. She was always trying to reform me, declaring that like so many comedians I had the nature of someone wrapped in a plaid on a Scottish crag waiting for doom. She was excited by events and pleasure. Nothing ever happened to me. If there was an earthquake I would have left before it began and returned to take down the accounts of eye-witnesses. I will probably die of boredom in extreme old age. Bonte insisted that I was indifferent to all that made life enjoyable. Look at me, going off where I was constantly in pain from bee-stings camped in the scrub with those oafs! Bonte came with me on one trip and was so gay and competent that she quite lit up the camp.

I came back from the city on one occasion bearing the records of Benjamin Britten's *The Rape of Lucretia* and nothing would suit Bonte but that we must set aside an evening to listen to it. Terry Ewen had dropped in to hear any news and found himself with Roddy and Mac on the sofa by the fire where they promptly all went to sleep. Bonte and I looked over while *The Rape of Lucretia* wailed on, and there was dear old Mac big and bolt upright, his eyes shut, Roddy asleep on his shoulder, and Terry snoring with his chin sunk in his checked scarf. We broke into yells of laughter which woke them.

"What a fuss to make about a bit of a do," was Terry's comment on the opera as he departed.

Terry and his wife, Sadie, moved to the city later where Terry sold landrovers and Sadie sold furs in a big store.

Sadie always won at the races and Terry always lost.

"Why do you take him if he loses?" I asked Sadie.

"Well, you couldn't go on your own."

"Why doesn't he bet on the horses you pick?"

"That's Terry." Sadie smiled.

Terry was full of complications and thoughts on religion, for he had once been a Catholic and an altar boy, and he had kindly impulses and generosity. He wanted to be a fisherman and go out on the snapper boats, but they all knew Terry would be no good at heavy lifting. He was a fascinating talker and, apart from women and religion, interested in doing what was correct.

"Well, I mean to *say*, I took Sadie to this nightclub all got up in the old fur, out for a night of glitter and splendour, and who do I find is running the place when we sweep in? Why, nobody but Chris whom I have known from way back! 'Terry, old man,' he says, seizing my hand, 'for you the best table! Do you remember the days when we cooked a saveloy over the gas-ring together in that crumby back room we were sharing and neither of us had a shirt to our backs?' Now I mean to *say*, in front of my guests when I was trying to look like a big-time operator this was a bit much. And he keeps darting back to our table with happy boyhood reminiscences about us doing a starve together and how we hadn't a shilling to put in the gas-meter. I can tell *you* it was a pall over the whole evening. 'Here he comes again,' Sadie would hiss. 'He's thought of something else.' A man doesn't want to be reminded amid wassail and song—he made me feel we were right back again with the old gas-ring."

Or his story might be: "There was a priest got into the cab the other day and it gave me a shiver just to see him as though I was back again with Brother Xavier wielding the strap. 'Father,' I says to him, 'do you really believe that when we die that there is this after-life?' And this priest just laughed. 'Ho, ho,' he said, 'what a fool I'll look if there isn't! Ho, ho, what a surprise I'll get!' And he hops out of the cab still laughing. Well I meanter *say*, when a man wants some information and all he gets is a gink that goes away *laughing* . . ."

Ernie shared in the new stir of life in Laurieton. The returned soldiers had built themselves a clubhouse and Ernie's contempt of those he termed "professional Returned Soldiers" did not prevent him from sampling its amenities. He always came in on Anzac Day to carouse a little. One Anzac Day his niece Dot called to me that she wished I would use my influence with Uncle. He was in no state to ride home.

"The horse knows the way," Ernie objected. He always left the horse in our yard. The sulky had fallen to pieces by this time. Over tea Ernie was gay and talkative. Roddy decided that he would really trounce Ernie this time at chess. He continued to ply Ernie with wine, meanly staying cold sober and even dropping a sleeping pill in the wine as he continued to lose. At midnight he had not won a single game and gave up in disgust, leaving Ernie ready to play and talk all night. He was gone before we were awake, taking a surf on the way to Dimandead. He said later that he had never felt better.

Dimandead, which could in the rain be all eroded cliffs and rain-soaked dirt, glowed the more splendid as we so often found ourselves cut off by the awful road. Ernie began to think we were seduced by the pleasures of gracious living, but our tastes had always been aboriginal— meals cooked over a wood fire, surfing, sunning.

He would be waiting for us at the week-end, coming out

now he was a little deaf and couldn't hear the truck, to stand by the broken fence where the cow had pushed through to eat Clara's roses. All that grew now were the pale pink Flowers of the West Wind thick in the grass by Ernie's boots that never wore out. We did not come. He would remind himself that he had never meant to stay at Dimandead. Any time he wanted he could just walk off. In Queensland he would meet old mates who had been in the great strike at Mareeba or mined out from Cloncurry. He was a free man who was not, as some people are, tied to a single place.

"A little spot of rain," he would say, coming into my kitchen, "hardly enough to wet the grass."

"Ernie, it was pouring. If we'd got out we would never have got back."

"You could go round by Moorlands."

"The bogholes on the Moorland road are worse. Benison was disappointed, too."

As Laurieton prospered as a tourist resort Dimandead, which was once expected to be glossy and lucrative, sank into wilderness. The beach track was now a system of revetments, deep holes, moats into which invaders had thrown boulders and tree-trunks in an often vain attempt to get through. When a city newspaper photographer came up to take pictures for an article a friend had written he was so keen to see Ernie and Dimandead that we enlisted Laurie Bucton, the butcher, and four strong men with Laurie's truck, known as the Maggot Waggon. With this task force to push when the Maggot Waggon was bogged, we struggled through, giving Ernie a great surprise. He posed with the goat or me patiently whenever Vic Johnson, the photographer, told him to, and Vic was enchanted by his beard, crouching round him at different angles and yelling, "Hold it!" or, "A little more to the left."

Vic had arrived on my doorstep in a downpour looking sad and grim as photographers usually do.

"Who do you think the editor is going to blame for the rain?" I greeted him.

"Me."

"Right. So you ring him up and tell him you have to stay until the weather clears up."

"He'll kill me."

I gave him a strong whisky which did his ulcers no good but made him feel happy. He rang the editor in an authoritative way and demanded an extra day. His orders had been to come the three hundred miles from the city and get back that night. Editors are like that. Vic did not get back for three days. He was a crack photographer and the scenery enthralled him, particularly Ernie. For years, when I saw him occasionally, he would ask after Ernie with the deep pleasure of a man who had found the Perfect Beard.

My old truck, which could no longer take the long distances up to New England, finally gave out, just managing to stagger back in one last faithful burst, collapsing at the door of Ken Nolder's garage at Kew seven miles from home. Trucks were dear and in those years not easy to come by. Roddy declared I must have a new one and after much consultation I applied for a Commonwealth Literary Fellowship, simply saying that I could not finish my book without a truck. The chairman of the Advisory Board was Vance Palmer, who knew the frustrations of a writer. I was given a fellowship and bought the truck. Nine months later a couple of red-baiting Members rose in Parliament and said the Fund was under Communist influence, and one claimed that I was a Communist using my fellowship to tour the country circulating propaganda. The Government had no right to bestow tax money on me.

Roddy and I had a hearty dislike for Communist tactics and regarded the party leadership as authoritarian and out of touch with political realities. Years before when hawking cabbages in Lithgow I had once paid over two shillings for "a ticket", which I never got, but it had been partly a gesture to my kind hosts. Also I was willing to join any organization to see how it worked.

Now I was furious. "If I hadn't spent the money," I growled at my husband, "I'd give it back."

"Why not?"

"We haven't that much."

"We'll raise it."

So we scraped the bottom of our bank balance, borrowed from my brother-in-law, and sent back a cheque exact to a penny. As this appeared to be the first time anyone could remember money being given back to the Government it created a stir in Parliament and the newspapers. The Member apologized to me in the House and repeated his former statement on the steps so that I could sue him for libel. To the annoyance of my tough city solicitor I accepted the apology and, to put an end to it, when the Prime Minister, who was chairman of the Fund, wrote me a handsome letter I accepted the money back. One newspaper which had rung up gave itself a full-page spread: "Author Sobs into Telephone when Name is Cleared". " 'Those who clothe themselves in honour often come to lack any other garment,' " I had quoted. I was not sobbing, I was gulping, trying to swallow a mouthful of dinner which the call had interrupted.

Ernie never felt the same towards our son, a healthy

and tranquil baby, as he had felt towards Benison who gave us so much anxiety. He sensed that, just as with Benison he had gained, with the boy he lost us. He had been working out a cunning scheme. Dimandead always offered what a man thought he wanted most. This was one of its grandest illusions. Now Roddy and Ernie were working out how Roddy could open a school at Dimandead. It would be for "difficult" children, unwanted children. Ernie had the manual skills and we could teach anything else they needed. He pointed out that while he could not sell us land there was no reason why he couldn't lease it to us. Somehow I never believed in this mirage because I knew that Dimandead would decoy us to itself and destroy us if we were committed. Ernie it never destroyed, keeping him as a pet the way terrible old ladies keep a pug dog. If we sank our future in Dimandead we would be the knights of San Merci wandering pale by the lonely sedge. But even I could almost see the long low buildings gleaming there.

Some people from the city had bought the Twomey house over by the lake for a holiday resort, and for a time their barge plied gaily from Laurieton. The man's wife fell ill and he left the house at Humbug. Fishermen stole everything in it and the house sank into the grass. Only a few stunted orange- and lemon-trees put out shoots nibbled by the wallabies. Years later you could hardly see that a house had been there.

While I was waiting for my son to be born I gave up bee-keeping trips and wrote a play, which won a competition sponsored by the Commonwealth Government. It was about Alfred Deakin and I had foolishly provided about twenty male characters, so that it was too expensive to act. I had suggested to Ella Brunswick that she could deliver the baby at home ."Oh no, you don't," Ella said promptly. "It would be different if you were a fisherman's daughter about eighteen. But I know *you*." So, complaining to Roddy of Ella's cautious nature, I set off for Melbourne, driving as far as Sydney and leaving Benison with my mother. I had to go to Melbourne about material for my play.

Driving home we stopped with a friend in Maitland, who was chief librarian, and I thought I should make arrangements with a doctor to come back there. Also he could tell me when the baby would be born. He said four months. "Get out!" I exclaimed. "You're not serious?" When I thought how I had nearly had to sleep in the park at Melbourne because I couldn't find any lodging and had been given a sofa by strangers and had trudged in the cold from one end of the city to the other I realized the baby had been very undemanding. He inherited all the gentler traits which had missed Benison, the female Napoleon, and later he became a musician.

When I left for hospital Roddy was still learning to drive the truck. After seeing him swipe off the school gatepost I insisted on driving myself to Maitland. Bonte was determined to wave my hair before I went and scattered her paraphernalia for the perm all over the kitchen. During this process there was some confused excitement outside. The living-room chimney had caught fire and they were keeping it from me. Bonte went out to see what was afoot and came back to ask, "Where is my neutralizing solution?"

"Was that it in the jug? I thought it was hot water and poured it into the teapot and drank it."

Bonte rushed to the telephone to call Ella.

"Where is she now?" Ella asked.

"She's in the kitchen laughing."

"Well, if it had been poison she'd be dead by now." Ella rang off, congratulating herself that she had refused to have anything to do with the birth of my son. Benison went with me to Maitland where I occupied myself cutting a long book which the publishers thought might get them into trouble with censors. I had to wait on Benison, who had caught influenza and gave it to me. I itched all over from the antibiotics pumped into me. I was so tired from being up all night that having a baby was secondary. I asked the nurse if I could take my detective story into the labour ward and she said it was all very well to be serene, but you could overdo it. Because I did not seem worried they left me there and I nearly had the baby by myself, seeing how long I could do without anaesthetic. I was discovered, however, and immediately rendered unconscious until the doctor could get there, spoiling my interest in having the baby by myself. I was going to show Ella I wouldn't have been any trouble.

Benison was very interested in the baby. "Kangaroos," she told a horrified elderly lady, "have a pouch outside them, but the baby came from a pouch inside my mother."

His father drove the baby home from Maitland with Benison and myself in attendance. It might have been the strain of the trip that sent him to hospital with a poisoned foot. He was there for weeks and I had to drive the thirty-five miles to Port Macquarie to see him with the baby sleeping tranquilly beside me in its basket. The road at that time was worse than a creek-bed with huge broken stones laid for repairs. Even after the headmaster returned he was still breaking out in the mysterious rash only kept down by Pop Slocombe's horse-goo.

People would say, "Ah, it's going about", when a

mysterious epidemic, nurtured by mosquitoes and sandflies in the mangrove swamps, struck the town. The dead fish drying along the river bank for bait were also blamed. I had battled against every infant ailment with Benison and now, with a new baby and a sick husband, it was time to beat a strategic retreat. My good friends in Head Office pointed out that there was an interesting old school in a waterside suburb of Sydney falling vacant, and Roddy was too ill to resist. Our children make cowards of us all.

"It's no use," Ernie told him, "she's made up her mind. When a woman makes up her mind the best thing you can do is give in."

On Christmas Eve I was myself swept into hospital by a doctor friend who had an imperious nature and took no notice of any patient's objections. Roddy returned to Laurieton to manage the move. He had instructions to bring down my orchids, but he was distracted by bumping the back of the truck when he was dumping garbage and he brought only a glossy Moreton Bay fig-tree in a tin.

He had long had an election-day feud with a Seventh Day Adventist who lived across the river. The Seventh Day Adventist would not leave his house until after sundown and would wait at the gate of the school until a minute past eight. Roddy and Peg, who acted as assistant poll clerk, would be making up their tally when the Seventh Day Adventist would come knocking at the door demanding the right to cast his vote. They were too good-natured to refuse him the ballot paper.

Now he came to buy my ducks, ten of them, and Roddy let him have them for two shillings each. The next day he was back complaining that as soon as he let the ducks out of the bags they had soared off back across the river. He had not known that I would not cut their wings. "And they came straight back in this direction," he said grimly. He did not actually accuse Roddy of training them to fly home but began peering under the house and in places where ducks might be concealed. Roddy, in a haughty and aristocratic way, gave him his pound back. I never found out what happened to the ducks, probably a fisherman ate them, but I like to think they continued up the river to the swamps where they would be safe.

Most of Roddy's transactions over the sale of furniture seemed to be in the same strain. Some he gave away, some mysteriously vanished. He packed the books carefully in great boxes, then left the house until the removalists cared to arrive some weeks later. If you are in hospital these things fall into proportion.

I was again stitched down the middle from one of the bargain-basement operations where doctors peer in and decide what to snatch. I had really thought I might die this time and my hidden motive was to bring the children where they would be near my mother and sister. But the Chinese declare I am under the sign of the Water Rat which can burrow, swim or run untiringly, while Roddy is the Wise Snake who shares the same burrow.

Before I had left I drove Ernie to Port Macquarie to draw his first issue of the old-age pension. "Now Royalty and I are on the same level," Ernie remarked. "The country's supporting both of us." The old-age pension, by his spare method of living, actually allowed him to save some money. For Ernie, accustomed to live on almost nothing, it was wealth.

"You'll never come back," Ernie had said on our last visit to Dimandead.

The others had gone down the beach and I was fretful because the food would be overcooked. I was inclined to be haggard at that time and impatient with Ernie. "We'll be back here every holiday, see if we're not."

And, indeed, for some years after we left we spent more time at Dimandead than when we were in Laurieton. We would come straight down the Moorland road and never go into Laurieton except for food and to see Bonte and Mac, who had retired from the post office to the cottages they let by the breakwater.

Ernie lived from day to day in enjoyment of his animals, his morning toast, the sunlight on the paddocks, the way a bird whistled back to him. He had immense reserves of the profound tranquillity of a meditative man. When he lay down at night and his thoughts swept over Dimandead where he knew which trees were budding, which insects breeding, it was as though the pattern of the place had become pattern of the man. He was Dimandead.

"I've often thought I'd go back to Queensland and have a look at a mine I never rightly tested out."

"Ernie, you need a drink." I shook the stone demijohn. "There's only a little in the bottom and it'll serve them right if they come back late and find we've drunk it." I tilted the wine into two enamel mugs and a little dead lizard fell out from the last of the wine.

"Clean little feller, ain't he?" Ernie poked the lizard reflectively. "Paws folded on his chest. When I die I'm going to walk out somewhere in the dunes with a rifle and the warm sand will drift over me."

"Drink up! Anyway, they wouldn't want any wine if they knew there was a lizard in it."

We drank our wine, toasting each other. "Here's seeing you."

I knew that when Ernie went in to town there would be no Rodds to press books on him. He would go past a house of strangers where no one would welcome him in. He had all of our friends, Rudl would play chess with him, Bonte and Mac would be glad to welcome him to a meal, and now he had many mates of his own.

But Ernie's waiting for us to come so stamped itself on my mind that I would always see him in the sunlight with the Flower of the West Wind around his boots, looking down the track, and Dimandead looking over his shoulder.

Chapter XI

No sooner were the Rodds gone than Clara came back. "It seems to be a law of nature," Ernie said. "A man thinks at last he's got a chance to catch on his loafing and before he knows it a woman has arrived thinking up things for him to do."

Later, Clara could only express what she thought of the house by a deep groan. But like the swallows who called in all their relations to help build the nest over Ernie's bed, Clara called in her clan and had new bearer beams under the kitchen floor, all the white-anted wood ripped out, the window replaced, the kitchen painted and new linoleum laid, a new stove and sink. Even the newspapers in the little room Benison and I had once occupied were ripped down.

Ernie took refuge in his bee-yard down near the lake in very thick bush and, with a series of good years, refurbished his hives so that there were again treacle tins full of dark honey. He refused to wear a bee veil and the bees would be hanging from his beard.

The white ants took refuge in our shack and my first thought when I came up was always to crawl under the house and look for white ants' nests. When Roddy hired some builders, at Bonte's instigation, to enlarge and extend the veranda, they built it low down to the ground, which made a perfect setting in the damp and dark for white ants to work.

This meant that we, too, had to tear down inner walls, put in new windows and floorboards. A wool expert, Jim James, master-minded this operation, insisting on aluminium frames for the windows which the white ants could not chew.

Ernie, creosoting the tank stand, was very witty about the white ants, telling us about the man who had left his suitcase standing in an upstairs bedroom of a Queensland hotel while he went down to do a little drinking. He changed his boots before he went and thought no more about it. When he came back he lifted up his suitcase and out fell a chunk of ant-heap where the white ants had eaten all his clothes. He lifted up his boots and the white ants had eaten the soles off. "Industrious little fellers," Ernie said affectionately, helping James to pull down the walls to get at them. They did not touch the great slabs of red mahogany but had built behind them so that we had an inner wall composed of white ants and the earth they had brought in. They chewed along the floorboards leaving a thin paper on top which a footstep would crumble. "These wet years," Ernie murmured, "the bees have done real well. Plenty of nectar in the blossom."

Terry, on holidays in Laurieton, somehow found himself involved in hammering and holding up wallboards. My friend Elizabeth cut her leg open in the surf and was driven in to the doctor to be stitched after she had insisted on bringing back her load of wood from the beach to mend floors.

It was a toss-up which would win, the host of friends or the host of white ants. Terry was still full of conversation and philosophy and sat in the lamplight talking about the after-life with Ernie, who didn't believe there was one, and Jim James, who didn't care but would take any side for the sake of argument. Years later, coming up with his family to Dimandead, James had a heart attack just as they were leaving, was whipped into Port Macquarie hospital and nearly found out about the after-life for himself. Dimandead had done for him what it did for everyone, given him an outlet for his energies until they tore him apart. After that, when he came to Dimandead, he took it much more quietly as Ernie had advised. James was going to finish the outdoor lavatory and roof it when he had his heart attack, so for the next ten years it didn't have a roof, and then a bushfire swept through and burnt it down.

Because we had to come three hundred miles on our visits we stayed much longer at Dimandead. One year we brought a clerical friend, the Reverend Alf Clint, who sat on the beach persuading Roddy it would be a good idea if I came with him to a small aboriginal mission far up on the Cape York Peninsula to write about a trochus and cattle co-operative he was forming there.

"What about the children?" I had just brought them back from Central Queensland on what was my last trip before writing *The Honey Flow*.

"You can take Bim," Roddy agreed generously, as though giving me some splendid gift.

By the time Bim was three Ernie was accustomed to look at him sternly. "He kicked his sister." I had never seen him so angry as on this occasion. "A boy who kicks his sister when—" he could not even contemplate such sacrilege. Had we not been there Ernie would undoubtedly have given Bim the licking he deserved and it would have done them both good. But Ernie restrained himself. I think that Ernie and Bim only became friendly when Bim was hitch-hiking to Queensland to look for work over the school holidays. He and an equally outlandish friend were heading for Mount Morgan and called in at Dimandead where Ernie insisted on giving Bim some money and advising him about Queensland. With his long hair and his guitar he was still strange to Ernie, but he was broke and looking for work, refusing to send home for money. That was something Ernie understood. Bim's friends, musicians, thought Ernie "cool". It was a high compliment. They found Dimandead a friendly refuge for young outlaws.

Alf Clint, one Sunday at Dimandead, decided to celebrate Mass on the kitchen table in our shack. He just put on his white alb over his shorts, brought out his little communion set, and placed a couple of candles in milk bottles. Ernie attended as an onlooker, sitting by the fire, interested, with his eye cocked like a bird in the clearing. Alf was accustomed to celebrate Mass on some lonely island, in thatched huts and native churches. Ernie could count on one hand the number of times he had been inside a church, but he formed a warm admiration for Alf. "The kind of bloke that anybody could get on with."

When we came back to Dimandead from the Torres Straits where we had left Alf, everything looked the same until we drove into our clearing. Across it was a hideous scar of upturned clay and turf where a tractor had churned its triumphant way across the paddocks, past our veranda and through the fence where Ernie had obligingly removed the wires to let it pass. He could not resist the plea of a fellow miner. It was his old principle of letting people have anything they asked, of giving the coat off his back.

"They'd never have got through the swamps," he explained. "You know that. Got to give a man a fair go."

There were notices on great stakes, claiming not only the sandhills but all the swamps behind and all up our creek.

I called in to a sherry party in the city and to my astonishment heard a dumpy little man, Sir James or Sir George Something, holding forth to a circle of ladies about his claim on fifteen miles of perfect beach and how by superhuman effort he had driven a road there and what an undependable lot the fishermen were as a work force.

"The first time I saw this place," he said, "I drove in my car to this farm behind the cliffs at Dimandead. No one there except an old chap with a beard puttering about. Over in a clearing is a run-down shack but nothing else. I just sat in the car and looked at it and a feeling like poetry came over me. 'This is for *you*,' I says to myself. 'Retire here, put up a good house and retire.' I'd let the old man stay on and potter about till he died. Just the place for me and the wife to breed cocker spaniels and grow banana-passionfruit. There's a market for them."

"Which?" I said stonily. "The banana-passionfruit?"

"The dogs." He was a good-tempered little man.

"That is my house in the clearing," I told him, "the run-down shack. Neither I nor my friend, Mr Metcalfe, who owns the three hundred acres, would sell you an inch of it."

The ladies hastily changed the subject.

My dramatic denunciations of rutile-mine-owners left Ernie undisturbed when I next came to Dimandead, but he hinted to the manager at the rutile works that I was getting more cut up than the clearing. It was time the rutile works built its own road. This they did, making a quarry of the south flank of Dimandead and throwing the rock and clay into the swamp. They brought in power lines. Tall corrugated-iron sheds hummed with machinery. Their dam cut off the water from the lagoon, and the dam, stagnant and scummed with oily sludge, covered our track to the beach so that we had to scramble round its edge.

The thunder of machinery as the rutile works thumped and roared twenty-four hours a day cut out the sound of the sea. The place spawned more buildings, it sprawled wider and wider. A dust cloud from the trucks hung over the plains of wildflowers. To widen the road into Laurieton the grove of redgums by Ernie's gate were nearly all chopped down. This was so the heavy machinery could be moved. The quarry in the south flank of Dimandead, which looked like a great cancer, eroded and began trickling down in bloodstained clay and yellow bile, leaking its wound into the dam and silting it up. In the golden lagoon were old motor tyres, rusted oil-drums, jutting iron and timber that washed out when the dam collapsed. Another dam, much deeper, with a huge fortification and a pump-house, was put up just below our house.

"In fifty years," Ernie comforted me, "it will all be gone."

"So will we. In the meantime these people have made something beautiful into a disease."

When I was bad-tempered because the beach blew away in fine stinging dust because all the heavy elements had been churned out of it, Ernie muttered as usual that it was "nothing a good storm wouldn't fix". As patron and saviour of the rutile works Ernie was always invited to the Christmas parties. Even Alan Mobbs was "working on the rutile" and Ernie knew all the men there.

I tried to take Ernie's view, and one year when our son was about ten he made friends with the manager's son and there were visits to our shack and we were invited to visit the rutile works roaring and churning by night, sifting down through great worms the gold and rutile and zircon. We stood on steel ladders in the noise while processes were explained to us. We were polite.

Next day we were driven down the beach five miles where a dredge in a small lake was chewing out sand dunes. The operator was tranquilly reading a book as he sat in the sun on the dredge. "Now there's a job I'd like," Roddy murmured.

But I was unreconciled and secretly uttered a great Scottish curse. It is the only time in my life I have ever cursed anything, believing that curses only ruin the one who curses. I cursed the rutile works for Dimandead, the great headland with its bleeding, cancerous erosion. I cursed the men's indifferent greed. It was all very well to say that "the Rutile" made work for the men of Laurieton. The men of Laurieton would boil down their grandmothers' bones if somebody paid them, as they would boil the bones of this land.

"May their gold go into the sea that it came from," I said. "May their roofs fall down. May they strike with a knife with no blade."

A useless and futile curse. The cow from the rutile works had a special taste for the Christmas bells which once grew in thousands on the plains and the flowers vanished into its great coarse mouth. The men went shooting kangaroos at the week-end. "Teach them to stay inside my fences where they're safe," Ernie said.

The Rutile budded a second diseased-looking set of excavations on the road to Moorlands, levelling great tracks of white paperbark swamp and leaving black sludge in their place with uprooted trees like skeleton corpses.

There was the year of the flood when the North Coast excelled itself in the continuance of rain. It drank it up until even the rutile works' road, built high over the swamps, was under water. In Laurieton the Camden Haven River, which had never flooded so near the sea, spread out over the low-lying land in rolling brown torrents.

Ernie had gone in to have Christmas dinner with Jack, who now lived in a house near the punt. Albert of the magnificent moustache, the courtly manner, the great maker of mead and honey beer, had died. Perhaps, although neither of them had ever been close to Albert, his absence reminded his two younger brothers that they had a stronger link with each other. Not that when they met at the hotel they said much. Jack was inclined to remark, "How's the *farm* going?" with the accent on the "farm" to remind Ernie of Jack's orthodoxy in putting fertilizer in the "furrers".

Jack had moved his circus caravan over to a grassy bank on the Dunbogan side of the river. He complained that in a storm the caravan did not just shake and tremble, "it cantered". He had cooked Christmas dinner for his brother, and Ernie duly appeared wading through the flood water. People were being taken off in boats from Dunbogan, near Jack, and moved to the higher ground at the foot of the Big Brother. Even Jack suggested to Ernie that perhaps they'd better shift.

"You invited me to dinner, didn't you? Damned if I'm going to shift before I've had it."

"That's right," Jack agreed. "Don't see how I'd eat all this tucker by myself. But you always was a selfish bugger. Probably get me drowned. Always trying to get me killed even when I was a little kid."

Complaining cheerfully he dished out the dinner, and the water, which had only covered the floor, crept up the table leg. They were sitting with the table top six inches out of the flood water as they finished their Christmas dinner. They did not hurry and they ate with appetite, swapping brotherly insults.

"How about the washing-up?"

"Be damned to the washing-up! All this flaming water."

They were taken off by boat as the water rose over the table.

The rutile mine changed hands once again. The dumpy little man had sold out to a syndicate and the syndicate sold out to the Americans, giving a party in a city hotel where the champagne alone cost hundreds of pounds.

The Americans had their own methods. They would come driving up in a fleet of great black cars, alight hurriedly and go about saying, "Sack that man." Even if, it was reported to us, the feller in charge was only a director's son-in-law he still had to sack someone to show he was on the job. Then the Americans would get back in their cars and drive away, and the manager would promptly rehire whoever had been sacked if he wasn't high enough up for the Americans to notice, and everything would settle down again, and the work of chewing up the landscape would go on.

Dimandead still offered yellow daisies of classical shape and soft leaves glittering, the stiff everlasting with grey leaves and pointed sepals, purple pea vine, the sarsaparilla leaves so sweet the old hands used them in their tea when sugar gave out. In the dunes the wire grass swept long fronds under the wind and the little birds ran almost invisible as if blown sideways. Green and scarlet rosellas flew through the she-oaks, purple snake-flowers reared their delicate triple tongues from furred brown sheaths. The wait-a-while vine and the prickly clubs of yellow flower in the rocks gave way to white spider lilies on the cliff slopes. Lantana invaded our track with pink flowers, and at the cliff foot, where poor old Baldy's skeleton had so long been a landmark to the fishing eagles, his skull had sunk into the maiden hair, pale violets grew through the empty eye-socket. One day we walked under a great arch of rainbow on the beach. The feet of rainbows often rested in our clearing as if it were their native place.

The Rodds still cooked over their open fire in billycans or in Ernie's camp oven. We had added a kerosene refrigerator when we left the school. Hail beat down a guttering, a bird flew through a shattered window, the white melaleuca crept to the doorstep. And when we came up we would sweep out, clear a little, repair. The silver house, weathered to a grey that was indistinguishable from the paperbarks, had its door painted blue. The door was never locked. As soon as we went away Dimandead would quietly remove the traces of occupancy. A bat moved into the chimney to be ejected when the Jameses came. Now Bim was old enough to bring his friends by himself. Benison and my friend Elizabeth and I would come. After an accident Roddy was no longer able to surf and he refused to make the journey. He sent a jacaranda tree to be planted down by the creek against the gap in the trees that showed the South Brother. "Tell Ernie," he said, "that when it flowers I'll make a trip up to see it." Ernie pointed out that cattle loved nothing better than a jacaranda tree, but he built a great fence round the tree and saw it had water in the drought.

We told an artist how to get to the shack, warned Ernie of his coming, drew maps. "Don't go down *that* road. It leads to the rutile mine. Take the turn to the left and you'll come to a gate with a sign that says, 'Private Property—No Trespassers'. Go right in. You can't see the shack for the trees until you get the car to the watercourse. Ernie has made a rock crossing, but be careful of the bump going down into it."

The artist took his family and set out. "We drove and drove over those terrible plains," he reported. "Night was falling and the children were frightened and we had to turn back." This piqued Ernie, who, when he came over to spend the evening, would seize his hurricane lantern to go home and exclaim dramatically, "Well—out over the terrible plains!"

"I want a horse," Benison said when she was an art student. "Princess is too slow and she tries to wipe me off on trees."

Ernie considered this. When he thought of a horse it was not like a city poet. He thought of horses individually as persons. "Now Don is a steady goer and he'll camp. You can walk right up to him. Princess has the speed, but, of course, she's a mare and wants a bit of notice taken. She knows you've got the bridle behind your back and you can see her saying, 'Oh, so he thinks he's just going to hold out a bit of bread, does he?' So you'll hold out your hand with the bread in it and she'll just blow on it to show what she thinks of you and off she goes." If he had heard of Cocteau he would have doubted if the feller had much experience of horses.

"I want a horse with some spirit," Benison said. "A

young horse. Princess is too old and cunning."

Princess knew enough to break into a shambling trot when she saw Benison coming. Princess was the leader of a small herd, the puntman's old horse, Peg Slocombe's piebald gelding, Freckles, meekly eating grass now that Peg had gone off to be married and had children. There would always be a few horses eating grass with them whose owners had begged the hospitality that Ernie never refused. At sight of Benison with the bridle they would all lift their heads and move off towards the wooded rises.

When Ernie suggested that the stock sales at Taree were the following Wednesday it was agreed that he should come and advise on the purchase of the horse. Benison, Elizabeth and Ernie, with myself as driver, set out through Moorlands, Ernie in the back seat, advising already. When we reached Taree he disappeared into his favourite hotel and we had difficulty winkling him out.

"Hurry, hurry!" Benison urged. "It will all be over."

"Plenty of time," Ernie protested. "There's another sale next Wednesday."

The stockyards on the edge of the town were rimmed by cars heating in the afternoon sun, their windows glancing back white rays. But the pens were shaded by trees and the horses and cattle stood tranquilly enough, all except one gelding with a white eye, pawing and snorting.

"Not that one," I stipulated.

The Jersey cows, with their fawn-coloured flanks and black muzzles, were so beautiful that I begged, "Ernie, couldn't we just buy a few? They could graze around the lake."

Ernie observed that women were unaccountable at sales. They'd come to buy a horse, hadn't they? Under the shade of a tin-roofed stand by the ring red-faced farmers and their stout wives bid with grim concentration for cows and the afternoon wore on. The prices were ridiculous. They rose only when the horses were led in. Ernie, who had been smoking tranquilly, was outbid each time. "Plenty more auctions," he murmured as the last horses were led out.

"It doesn't matter." Benison was resolutely bright.

I looked down at her bent head. "Which one did you really want?"

"That one." It was, of course, the gelding with the rolling eye.

The horses were being loaded by a dealer who was taking them to the tablelands. In my travels I had learnt that a horse-dealer would sell his mother if you gave him a little over the last bid.

"I'll give you two pounds to boot for the gelding."

"Sold," said the horse-dealer promptly.

It was a dark bay verging to black, with a flowing mane and tail, and came from Moorlands. Its previous owner would truck it home for us to the butcher's paddock there. Benison could ride it down next day. When the horse was released in his home paddock he kicked up his heels and set off contemptuously to eat blackberry bushes at the far end of the slope. His day had been ruined by a senseless journey to a place he regarded with distaste. Now he intended to turn his back on human smells and recover his nervous tone.

Ernie was stirred by these unaccustomed stock dealings. "I've got three old horses just stumbling around the paddocks ready to drop in their tracks," he told the butcher briskly. "It'd be a kindness to them to get rid of them." The butcher made a deal to remove the horses and slaughter them.

He forgot about it for a few weeks and then he appeared one night and said he had come for the horses. In the meantime Ernie had seen Princess standing up to her knees in the lake with Freckles and the other old gelding, Sailor. His heart misgave him. "They can still pick a bit of grass," he thought. "They're still getting a bit of enjoyment."

When the butcher appeared Ernie denied absolutely that he had said anything about disposing of any horses. "Turning up here in the middle of the night," he told the butcher. "You must be drunk." The butcher wasn't speaking to Ernie for a long time.

"What is his name?" Benison asked the butcher's wife, as she gazed after her horse.

"Pickles—you can always catch him with a bit of bread."

We did not dare ask why Pickles was being sold. We found out. He seemed to prefer women as more likely bread givers.

"He tosses off boys," Benison said with satisfaction.

Pickles reminded me of my mare Betty who was always going back to Moorlands to look for her long-lost colt. They could have been of the same strain. Pickles had a hard mouth and a strong will. You could certainly catch him with bread, but the trouble was to find him. He took over the leadership of the herd from Princess and would lead them to some inaccessible gully. He objected to being parted from his herd. Benison adored him and easily foiled his attempts to buck and rear her off. She would go up to Dimandead without me just to ride the horse.

Ernie came to Sydney sometimes to play chess with Roddy and sample the pleasures of the city, but he complained that the smog gave him bronchitis. "I come down

123

here stomping like a two-year-old and before I know it I'm coughing my head off."

His curls were grey now, his pointed beard was grey. But his step was as light as ever. Aristocratic old ladies of Hunter's Hill who snubbed everyone who had not lived there for twenty years positively flirted with Ernie. With Roddy's white silk scarf about his throat, he would greet them with the courtesy of the ancient world. The barmaid also asked after him when I met her in the hairdresser's shop.

Once, strolling through the city on a solitary sight-seeing, he stopped to light his pipe and a business-man came up and pressed money into his hand. "God love you, old-timer," the man said. "It does me good to look at you." Ernie gracefully thanked him for the few shillings he did not need. He took the token as it was meant, for goodwill. As he moved through these haggard people, scurrying and perhaps overburdened, Dimandead looked through his eyes, with its eternal dignity. "It's the beard," he chuckled, but it wasn't the beard.

He sometimes stayed with a wealthy business-man, one of his nephews who was proud of him and admired him. His great-nephew John was grown up now, the little boy with red curls. Ernie visited. He enjoyed a meal of bean shoots and curious vegetables cooked at our house by a Chinese doctor and his wife who were friends of Benison. He took over the "fiddle" which had been bought for our son, who preferred a guitar. Ernie carried the fiddle back to Dimandead where he played jigs in the lamplight, old forgotten country tunes, from the days when he danced.

A professor of music from Melbourne on holidays in Sydney asked what she could play him on our piano and he said, "Well, there was one tune I always liked." He seemed almost shy.

"What was it?"

"It's called 'Danny Boy'." She played the Londonderry Air while he accompanied her on Bim's "fiddle":

... 'Tis you must go and I must bide—
But come you back when summer's in the meadow ...
Or when the valley's hushed and white with snow ...

But he had never gone back to Bertha, who married another man.

Ernie's visits were infrequent. He would just appear at the front door without warning. In 1965 he found that there was a free pass to the city for the old soldiers so that they might march in that special Anzac Day procession. He came down to visit us, on the free pass. He had so little intention of marching on Anzac Day that he had not even brought his returned soldier's badge. Over Ernie's protests Roddy rang the committee, who arranged for a car to come and pick him up.

We were delighted to see him riding near the front of the procession and he had a glorious time after the march, feasting with good fellows. He was returned home very drunk—not that it showed. He still spoke most lucidly and walked in a straight line, but there was a certain air of dishevelment about his beard. There is always some moral disapproval about returned soldiers drinking on Anzac Day, but for men who remember their near escapes from death and the queer and sinister chances of war, this is a defensive measure, a natural thing. What else can a man do?

But men at whiles are sober,
And think by fits and starts,
And if they think, they fasten
Their hands upon their hearts.

Now that Benison had the horse Pickles she coaxed our friend Margaret, a novelist and critic, to go to Laurieton by train, taking the bus from Kendall, then a taxi from the town. Margaret had never, in Australia, left the city. She came from Scotland. "But I have never been in the bush," she protested.

"It's not isolated," we assured her. I was to come up a week later by car. "Ernie has a motor scooter now and he often goes in to Taree to terrorize the traffic. His nephew Bert and his wife have come to live at Dimandead and Clara has gone in to Laurieton to be near the doctor. Bert would bring out your food because they go in to play bowls. Around the bend of the creek is the rutile mine, but luckily you can't see it."

Margaret and Benison went to Diamond Head and Benison spent all her time looking for the horse and riding it when she found it. Margaret called Bert in to deal with the refrigerator, which was as sensitive and difficult as Pickles. She took out all the food from the cedar cupboard with the mousehole gnawed in the door. She spread clean paper on the shelves. She had a wash-up of blackened billycans and frying-pans with all the odd plates and cups guests had left over the years. She carried mattresses on to the veranda and aired them, rigged mosquito nets. Competently she swept.

Benison suggested she should go for a walk over the plains.

"Where are they?" Margaret gazed doubtfully at the ring of trees about the clearing.

"Over there." Benison swept a careless arm half round the compass and Margaret decided to clean out a cupboard the white ants had chewed.

She felt, I think, that the trees were creeping nearer,

waiting to wipe her and the shack off the clearing as though they were writing from a wall, the quivering wall of sunlight on which is written, *"Mene, mene, tekel, upharsin."*

No two people ever have the same experience of Dimandead because they take their own events with them. Benison's event was being thrown from her horse and staggering home very little damaged. Most people become adjusted to the lawful peace of the place, its suggestion that one must give way to the inevitable until the inevitable is no longer there. Margaret, a competent person, was tested in this pride in her capability. As she and Benison sat by night at the table Margaret said, "I wonder if there's enough kerosene in that lamp?"

Benison, to be helpful, unscrewed the brass knob from the hole into which kerosene was poured and put in her little finger to feel the level. "I can't get my finger out," she said.

"Nonsense," Margaret said briskly. "Try again, Benison."

"It's stuck." Under the rim were jagged teeth of metal pointing downwards. Benison's finger when they both tried their best to tug it out was cut and bleeding. "Do try again."

"I can't. The finger's swollen."

Benison remained cheerful and courageous. So did Margaret, but this was a situation she was not trained for in Scotland. How did you get a finger out of a lamp? They set off in the darkness to go for Ernie. He had lived for a time in Clara's house with Bert and Bert's wife, but, finding the house too civilized, had moved down to the camp he had built for himself near the bees. It was sheltered there, he said, from the wind. He could lie on the hessian bedstead he had constructed with saplings and toss a piece of wood on the fire without getting out of bed at night. I think he liked the birds around his door, the little lake to which the ducks were coming back—but this was a secret between himself and Benison—"Tell everybody and they'll be in here shooting." Perhaps the blue lilies might come back, he thought, but they never did.

Benison, attached to the lamp, went sure-footed across Ernie's little plank bridges over the black ditches. A light rain was falling. Margaret followed uncertainly while patches of deeper darkness rose and crashed away as cattle. The two seekers-for-help toiled up the rise to Ernie's door. The motor scooter stood under a tarpaulin in a lean-to beside his little hut. He usually went to roost now at the same time as the fowls. "Wasn't he cold down there?" visitors would ask. "What, with a six-cat blanket?" Ernie responded.

Now, although it was only half past seven of winter darkness, Ernie was in a sound sleep. He thought he was being awakened in the middle of the night. He entertained Margaret and Benison with stories of queer accidents that had happened in mining camps or to men he knew who had been navvying or down the Darling. But he was unable to get the lamp off Benison's finger.

There was nothing to do but wait until Bert and Lois came back from the bowls club, which they were supposed to do about eleven at night. Ernie went back to sleep and Benison and Margaret returned through the dark and the falling rain. Margaret spent her time until eleven wondering if the finger would develop gangrene or fall off. She attacked the lamp with a tin opener, a chisel, a hammer. It seemed to be made of the kind of metal they use for interplanetary rockets. She couldn't even dint it.

At eleven o'clock they set off to consult Bert and Lois, who were concerned, amazed, but failed to find any solution. "Even the doctor," Bert said gravely, "wouldn't be able to prise the thing off with his tools. You'll have to go down to the rutile works in the morning and see if they've got the gear for the job."

Margaret spent a terrible night, waking every half-hour to bathe the finger with cold water. Benison, accustomed to strange happenings, slept.

In the morning they took the track by the creek, picking their way over eroded clay and broken trees until they came to the quarry and the bridge that the rutile works had flung across the creek to bring rocks for their roads. The two wandered into the manager's office where everyone from engineers to truck-drivers gathered to study the problem.

Under the supervision of the manager they cut round the lamp until it was only a jagged frill. Then they tackled the slow, painful job of removing the brass rim, which was now embedded in Benison's finger. Very gently, very skilfully this was accomplished.

Benison was driven in the manager's car to the doctor. In a week her finger was half-way down to its normal size. When we arrived we heard the story in three different versions. I owed the rutile works grateful thanks, and as I scraped white ants' nest under the house, I wondered how to say, "We have avoided you for years with your immense resources, your destruction and efficiency. Now that destruction has been turned to a small useful purpose. We thank you."

But they were still the enemy. I realized that the rutile works, a cancer in the side of Dimandead, had done something worse to me. It had made me mean. Thanks stuck in my throat. Benison was off looking for the horse as cheerful as ever. Margaret went around singing little songs in praise of rutile mines which were inhabited by angels of mercy. Oh hell, let them have the whole damned beach!

Some months later we were at Dimandead again and I was saying to Elizabeth as we went in to town for supplies, "Do you think we'll ever coax Margaret back again?" Elizabeth thought not. As I put the car into gear after we went through the gate nothing happened. I tried again, but although the engine was running the car did not move. We had a broken back axle.

There was nothing to do but walk down to the rutile mine to ring a garage. They had the only telephone for seven miles. Unfortunately, the people at the manager's office said, the line had blown down in a gale the night before. "There's always something. Talk about the trouble we've had!" The linesman had gone out to look for the break, but it might be hours before he found it.

I thought of Ernie saying, "Nothing that a good storm wouldn't fix." Dimandead fought back against the rutile works. First, they said, their dam had been swept away, then the road sank into the swamp. The cost of maintaining the road was terrible. Here the seas raced up to destroy, there the plains.

Elizabeth started in to Laurieton on foot. Benison went on the horse. I was left to telephone when the line was repaired. Long before that a great and costly car came racing across the bumps and hummocks of the paddock into the clearing.

"I'm Sloane," the man in it said. "They only just told me you had a broken axle. Get in."

"How did you know where my house was?"

"I ought to know this place. Years ago when we only

had two jeeps we had a terrible time. We couldn't get in to the creek. Ernie told us to cut through your clearing. We always owed you a debt of gratitude for that. I don't think we could have made it without."

We overtook Elizabeth on the plains and when she stepped into the car a cloud of flies came with her. Benison was taking the short cut so I left a message with the puntman, "If you see a very small girl on a horse would you tell her not to bother about the rear axle?"

The garage at Laurieton had a rear axle but no sleeve bearings. The rutile works manager drove me another five miles to the next garage. Finally a red-headed boy in a tow-truck came out and the car, looking somehow shameful, was upended and jolted away.

I realized as we settled into the life of the green clearing that I no longer felt mean and vindictive towards the rutile works. Along the creek came a faint roar which was either surf or the works chewing up and spitting out sand. After I was dead the great grey sheds would fall to rust, the sand dunes would sweep over the abandoned bulldozer, the machinery would fall into the grass. It is no use coming to a beautiful place if your state of mind does not match it. By an effort I felt benevolent towards the rutile works. One must clear and improve one's attitude against resentment. One must co-operate with the inevitable until at last the inevitable disappears.

Chapter XII

Bert and Lois had come to live at Dimandead to look after the old folk, full of good intentions, energy and cheerfulness. Lois set about establishing the wall-to-wall carpet from her suburban home, the vases of artificial flowers, the chenille bedspread. She improved on her mother-in-law's housekeeping and, presently, finding there was not enough work for two women in the house, Clara moved into a house of her own next to Dot in Laurieton. Her sight was beginning to fail, but she managed everything for herself and at ninety-two was still as quick to enjoy as when she had once climbed down the cliffs with me.

Bert established a garden for vegetables and fruit. He grew enormous papaws that looked as though they had been polished every morning, and no animals ever broke into Bert's garden. The agricultural strain in the Metcalfes, released in him after so many years of being adroit and affable, now flourished in bananas and oranges, in perfect tomatoes, in carrots with never a weed in the furrows.

We came up to find that past our fence a great wind-row of melaleuca and gum-trees had gone down before the bulldozers and in the torn-up quarter of a mile over to the rutile works stood naked poles bearing the wires for Lois's light and power.

"Whatever it cost us," Lois said with the air of a martyr, "it was worth it." Now she could have television, an electric stove and refrigerator. She was a tall woman with long legs and clear green eyes, self-confident as women are who are admired for their good looks. "Oh, Uncle and I understand each other, don't we? He knows I'm only joking."

After some time of Lois's gaiety Ernie decided that yet one more bloody woman had moved in on him. He built himself the corrugated-iron shack with a mud floor down near the bees, above what had once been his terraced vegetable garden by the lake. Bert and Lois felt humiliated by this. Not all their pleading could move his good-humoured determination to go his own way and they finally had to be content with persuading him to share one good meal a day.

"He's such an obstinate old devil," Lois complained. "Whatever you say he takes no notice."

She had come prepared to cosset him and do everything for his good. Now he would go off on his motor scooter for a trip around the tablelands of a few hundred miles, camping as he had done when he was younger. He would go off to the Returned Soldiers' Club in Laurieton and, coming home in the dusk, skid on the loose gravel and take a fall, sneaking home like a boy determined not to let the women know.

When he broke his collar-bone in a slight mishap with a car in Taree his first thought was that Lois must not hear of it. "Don't tell her," he persuaded his rescuers, but the bush telegraph had worked before Ernie arrived back. "And so you weren't going to say anything, were you?

You thought I wouldn't find out? Really, Uncle, the things you get up to, I wonder at you."

On one occasion when the motor scooter just brushed a motorist's mudguard Ernie had given the motorist a lecture. "I was riding a bike before you were born." He didn't say that it was a push-bike. He was tetchy about pedestrians who were irresolute. He had puttered into Taree and was waiting at a crossing for a nervous man who kept advancing and retreating. Finally he lifted the front wheel of the scooter and brought it down on the man's toe. "Let that teach you to make up your flamin' mind," he roared.

The constable at Moorlands had been dubious about giving Ernie a licence. He thought he was too old at seventy-five. "Where did you learn to ride it?" he asked. Ernie told him he had ridden the scooter around the paddocks over the furrows. "Well, look," the constable told him, "take the bike into Taree and if you come back alive I'll give you a licence."

So Ernie rode the dangerous dirt roads around Dimandead which the Rutile had laid down for trucks, and when he broke the couple of ribs he was persuaded, scolded, pleaded with to lie still and not breathe too deeply. Lois had once worked in a hospital.

"Now that is not the way Nature works," Ernie jutted his beard at her. "Stands to reason the lungs want to push out against the ribs and they should be expanded."

So he bought himself a flageolet and the defiant tootling drifted across the paddocks, startling the hares in the dew. He was curing himself in his own independent way. "Cantankerous old devil," Lois said. Men must be cajoled, bullied, jollied into right behaviour, and Ernie was impervious to all she had in her feminine weaponry.

The contest between them settled down to resignation on Lois's part. "Just let him go his own way," Bert advised. "Uncle's always done what he liked. He's too old to change now." Bert, too, had looked forward to working with Uncle, sharing with him, and Uncle had withdrawn into his independence.

When they found that the object of their care had betaken himself to his disgusting corrugated-iron shed down in the scrub, a dwelling that would disgrace even an aboriginal settlement, Bert and Lois began to experience a peculiar desolation. Bert, with all the digging, hurt his back. Lois for a time had to go into hospital. And their pride and good nature had suffered other hurts. Ernie was no Lear of the plains, ousted from a comfortable home by those who had dispossessed him. He rather enjoyed his contests with Lois.

Now he felt freer to come and go. He let the great ditches silt up because the lake was coming back. He still repaired his fences, burnt off the underbrush skilfully. Dimandead was like a great park.

We, too, pleaded with him to take our shack in the clearing. "Not on your life! I'd just have settled in and you'd be coming back again. Too much trouble moving in and out."

So he stayed in the honey-scent by the lake taming birds, playing his flageolet or the violin. An Indian summer had set in for Ernie. He had a little loosed the ties of Dimandead. He went back to Queensland on a wide-flung tour with Alan Mobbs in Alan's old car, revisiting all the places he had known. But somehow his old mates were dead or they did not remember. He came back to Dimandead without the new pair of Queensland leather boots. Leather was not what it was and the old boots had not worn out yet. Speeding through Queensland by car—his hearing was not so good and his eyes did not take in the rapid blur of the roads—was not the same as travelling slowly in the sulky with a good horse. Old Princess, indestructible, was still stumbling around the paddocks, bullying the other horses now that Benison's horse, Pickles, had gone.

"Every holiday Pickles gets wilder," Benison had complained as Pickles scampered off tossing his mane. "If I had him in Sydney I could ride him oftener and then he wouldn't be so hard to catch."

There was nowhere we could lodge a horse in Hunter's Hill. Roddy, with one arm, was editing and typing book after book. Bim was studying and playing. Benison was working in an electrical engineering factory and painting pictures in a studio built at the back of the house. Elizabeth and I at week-ends scoured the countryside for a hundred miles round Sydney. Finally we bought an old dairy farm of several acres in a little valley in the Blue Mountains, and a paddock was constructed for Pickles, with a stable which he treated with disdain. He was not used to shelter and would stand out in the most terrible weather in his horse-coat, refusing to go into the stable.

The first problem had been to get him from Dimandead to the Blue Mountains. Benison was determined to ride him down herself. "You'd have done it," she told me.

"I'd sooner ride a mad elephant than Pickles. I wouldn't even ride him round the paddock."

The problem was solved by the artist who had once lost his way on "the terrible plains" looking for Dimandead. "Nothing simpler," he declared. "There's my son, Jonathan, who was studying singing in Adelaide. He's at home eating his head off. He'll ride the horse down."

Jonathan, a wild good-natured boy with a beard, was

willing. He stayed at the house in the clearing for several days trying to catch Pickles until Ernie walked over with a bit of bread and put the bridle on him. Then there was the epic struggle to accustom Pickles to the idea of Jonathan's riding him. The Rodds were able to track Pickles and Jonathan down the coast by reports in newspapers and from radio stations. A young man with a beard, stripped to the waist and singing as he rode, was not inconspicuous.

There were long periods of silence, never explained, when Jonathan had lost Pickles. Benison fretted. Jonathan looked for the horse.

Weeks passed. At last a telegram from Jonathan sent Benison up the mountains to wait for him. She lived alone on the farm in a fever of impatience. She was perfectly capable of living by herself in lonely places.

When Jonathan handed over the horse he told her that going to Dimandead and riding the horse back had changed his life. "After that I realized I could do *anything*." Benison begrudged him the journey. He set off for Greece with his pay for the ride and I reflected that it had cost me more than I had paid for Pickles in the first place.

Pickles was as independent as ever after his adventures. He would rush up the paddock neighing at sight of us, waiting for Benison to fling on the saddle and take him out. But he found the weekdays boring by himself. He set his mind to breaking out and heading back north. He always went north and would be recaptured at the edge of some great gulf of air where the cliffs fell hundreds of feet, and even a horse as spirited as Pickles found this great ditch of the Grose Valley too wide by miles to jump.

One time some irate householder tied him to a telegraph pole and left him there all night in the storm. I rode him home and he was glad to go, but planning to get back to the paddocks of Dimandead. I would have done anything to bring this about, for I had so thought myself into the horse's skin that I suffered.

"He needs other horses," Benison said, and a woman who had other horses took him as part of her riding school. Pickles was very happy. But the horsewoman had to break up her riding school and offered to sell Pickles to a good owner. Sooner than leave him alone on the farm we agreed. But I was still haunted by the idea of Pickles far from home and setting his nose north to the unattainable paddocks of Dimandead. This is the curse of animals, that you become their jailers and then their slaves.

Ernie approved the farm high in the mists. He knew he could always go there if he wished to annoy Bert and Lois, but he agreed with my neighbour in the mountains that the place was all right if you didn't mind winter nine months of the year. Ernie was too good-natured to really want to spite Bert and Lois. He knew their goodwill. He returned to Dimandead appreciating the warmth of his snug little corrugated-iron shed in the hum of the bees.

Now Benison had no horse at Dimandead. "Far better if you'd left him here in the first place," Ernie said.

"But I couldn't catch him."

"Well, that's the way of horses. They see no reason to be rode. And, come to that, what were we given feet for?"

I had worried about that horse for so long I tried to forget him. At least he had not succeeded in killing either Benison or Jonathan. But I was haunted by the vision of a reproachful horse far away among strangers. Now the sheer impossibility of tracing him defeated me, for Benison's horsewoman friend had moved and left no address.

The horse had come to symbolize something for me in a way that Ernie might perhaps have understood. All of us have some sore place in our mind and mine has to do with ill-treated animals or children.

At this time I had struck what Ernie called "a bad spell" of too much work and not enough laughter. In this turmoil it was easier to go to the mountains, only seventy-five miles away, than to Dimandead, though the road had been shortened and was a faster road than it had been when it took us all day in the dust to arrive. All the time the children were growing up we had fought through floods and heat to get to Dimandead. It was Benison's spirit place, the land of her dreaming, as the aborigines would understand.

I had mixed the ideas of loneliness, desertion, Ernie, Dimandead and the horse. Somewhere I had made a pattern in my mind in which I had done the wrong thing. Where did it begin? I had left Ernie lonely. I had left the horse lonely and I was powerless to do otherwise. As it was, I thought defensively, I was always in three places at once, the busy water-rat, running, swimming, digging and climbing in the publishing game which is of all the most maddening. Or an overburdened horse plodding on until it dropped. I always needed guilt and self-reproach to make me work.

In my life of telephone calls and letters, of reading manuscripts and publishing, I came to answer the front door, and there was Ernie with his little suitcase such as children take to school.

"Ernie!" I cried, hugging and kissing him and burying myself in the beard, gold-stained from smoking. "How wonderful!" Ernie accepted the family rejoicings and, when they died down, the impression just drifted casually that he had not told Bert and Lois he was coming. He had to go to hospital. Bit by bit it transpired that he had a lump that the local doctor said was cancer. Bert and Lois would have made a fuss. If he had to go to hospital he'd sooner be in Sydney.

Telegrams and letters went to Bert and Lois. What had saved them from an ignominious retreat from Dimandead was not only their own definite and determined natures but that they had discovered a new rich life. Before they broke up their home in the city they had thought bowls was a game for elderly dodderers. Now they had become champion bowlers winning prizes and pennants and cups and fleeing from Dimandead three days a week to play in tournaments.

It was a sight to see Lois and Bert setting off in their car. Bert, in particular, was glorious in knife-edged, snowy flannels, his club blazer with the crest on the pocket, his panama hat with crest on band. His hair was brilliantined, his moustache had an air of authority and anticipation. Lois, more tall than ever in white, more athletic, had the endurance, the determination, the strong wrist and flexibility of a champion.

Ernie had just waited until they went off to bowls and then vanished. He and I went together to wait in the loathsome disinfectant smell at Sydney Hospital while the doctor examined him.

"He says it's ray treatment or the knife," Ernie recounted. "I said, 'The knife.'"

Cancer was eating into Ernie as the rutile mining ate into Dimandead. He had this lump in his back. He was no whit disturbed but as humorous as ever. When I went to bring him home from the hospital he made a royal progress. All the other patients had to come and wish him well, swearing undying friendship. Nurses kissed him, doctors left their busy round to shake his hand. He was something fabulous and precious, he was their country, strong and wild and strange.

He was no sooner established in bed at our house than, waiting to give me the slip, he had dressed himself and walked a mile down to the hotel by the water. The barmaid greeted him as a long-lost friend. When I realized he had gone out by himself I knew how Lois must feel.

"Ernie, you *know* that I would have driven you. To climb that great hill coming home when you were only just out of hospital!"

"Man needs a bit of exercise," was all that Ernie would say. He complained that, as usual, Sydney had given him "a cold". It was a bad attack of bronchitis and Roddy just called in the doctor who ordered him to stay in bed. When he was able to sit on our patio a group of visiting ladies asked him whether he should not give up smoking. "I realize smoking may carry you off," said Ernie, straight-faced. "I've been smoking since I was ten and I'm seventy-nine now. It'll take me any day."

Elizabeth and Benison and I drove him to Dimandead. Roddy, who had played unending games of chess with him, saw him go with foreboding. I drove very carefully and Ernie, in the back, was quite himself, pleased to be going back to Dimandead. But as soon as he had established himself in his hut he lay in bed. "Just that damn cold I always get in Sydney. Can't seem to shake it off."

"The obstinate old devil," Lois cried, with tears in her eyes. "He worried us sick. We're so relieved to have him back I can't tell you."

I was determined that when we went Ernie should move into our shack. "It's sheltered there, Ernie. You'll be closer to Bert and Lois, and Bert can come across and see if you need anything instead of tramping all this way. I'll come down and take your things up in the car."

"Don't you do anything of the sort. I'll bring my own gear."

I was so pleased to have persuaded him to move into our house that I conceded this. Early next morning, while we were packing the car to leave, Ernie appeared on the other side of the stream. He had his great miner's barrow piled as high as his head with his goods, tucked neatly under a tarpaulin. He had even roped on the top his shovel and pick and the blackened camp oven he had carried all over Queensland. He had pushed this load near half a mile around the lake over tiny plank bridges above his ditches, through the paddocks to the new horse-gate he had built in our fence for the lost Pickles.

Our outcry only made him smile. "Just like women," he said, "carrying on a treat at a man for walking across his own paddicks. The barrow was humping the load."

We kissed Ernie and left him, and he settled in contentedly by the fire. He could lean out of bed to put wood on it in the night if he chose. Bert found him in the morning lying cold on the floor. He had got out of bed in the night and had a stroke.

In the hospital they gave him little hope, but after months he was back at Dimandead again, and when we arrived he walked across the paddocks to meet us. His smile was a little stiff on one side, but he walked. He sat down by the fire just as usual, yarned of the old days in Queensland. Bert and Lois had established him in the old laundry across the yard. He could make himself a cup of tea on the primus, sit on the sunny doorstep and talk to the cats.

When I went there and saw the tiny window covered in cobwebs and black spiders I made to brush them away.

"You leave them alone," Ernie said with spirit. "Those spiders are doing a fine job keeping the miskeeters off me. Never can let an animal or insect alone but must always take a swipe at it! They've got their life, I've got mine."

For two—was it three?—years, Ernie lived in the tin laundry. Bert waited on him devotedly. He and Lois still went into town three days a week to play bowls, and Ernie's relations reported that he sometimes said, when he came into town, that he'd like to go to an old men's home where he'd have plenty of people to talk to. But no old men's home would have had him because he was too ill.

At last Bert and Lois could justify themselves by caring for him. When we came we would drive him about and he even took himself to the hotel for a drink, meeting Jack, hale and discontented as ever. Ernie was like an old dog who has always had his own kennel and will not go into the polished house, but in summer the little laundry was very hot and in winter very cold.

Alan Mobbs and his nephew, Harry Metcalfe, visited him. Bim and his friends dropped in and played their guitars. He liked that and wished they would come more often. The rutile works spread its depredation all over the plain, and the hidden death in Ernie kept pace.

There was an incident. People said it was a good thing Lois had got the gun away from him. Ernie would have thought it was just her need to interfere. Ernie had often told Roddy he would die when he chose and find a clean, warm sandhill for his bones. His plans for his end had been thwarted. A woman as usual. Doing things for your good.

"If it was that old rifle he used to have," Harry Metcalfe told me, "I doubt if he could even hit himself. It was all out of kilter. Once Ernie fired it and it hit a bough yards off where he reckoned to make his mark. And if it was his service revolver I doubt if he had the ammunition."

The James family went up for a holiday and reported that Ernie was lonely. "I think he wants you, but he's too proud to say so."

"Just as soon as I finish this book I'll be up there." The book had taken me three years and I was within a week of the end. I had written to Ernie: "Hang on. We're coming."

But I had delayed too long. He did not eat anything and was slowly starving to death. He did not like being dependent. As the white ants slowly ate away the walls of a house so the virus in him left only the resolute set of his great arched nose, his amused eyes, his independence and the skin that covered him.

He had long ago let the rutile company have his two-hundred-acre lease on the plains. "They need it more than I do. Bert don't want grazing. He's got enough here without it."

The rutile company had even taken a miner's right to prospect over our clearing and Ernie's bee-yard. He smiled as he thought of my language. "Won't she perform!" I was not able to come up and fight them in the warden's court because of the book.

He knew then that he would die without us. He sat in his door in the cool after the sun went down and could see, with dimmed eyes, the trees crowding down the slope from the cliff towards Bert's vegetable garden with its great defences and high wire-netting.

Because the trees didn't have a human time-scale nobody remembered they were alive. Come to that, if an angel got itself up in green feathers and just stood there, nobody would notice. Or if it put on coloured feathers and flashed across the clearing—just a bird. His mind ranged over Diamond Head from the gate on to the road up the track, through the timber and the high rock pinnacles. He knew what was growing in every crevice, he didn't need to see it any more.

Ernie thought it was a pity that the rutile works hadn't found any rutile on his property. They would have driven through with their great mechanical scoops and levelled all that scrub down by the bee-yard that the Rodds set such store by. You had to clear the land. He'd always held to that. Bert would never sell but would pass the land on to young John. Bert had been upset when he found empty shells just inside the gates because he set store by the kangaroos and birds. Ernie's great-grandfather had come to Australia for taking a bird on private property, and now here was his great-great-grandson protecting birds on private property.

Ernie wished that Benison would come with her eager talk. They had been talking to each other since she was a little nugget of a baby. His arms that had been knotted and brown were now mere driftwood. All his strength had fallen from him. Well, he was on the edge of eighty-three and when a man could not eat it stood to reason that Nature had only one thing left to take away—his life. Not that he had ever valued it. He slept a little. He waited.

"I can't stand it any longer," Lois said determinedly one morning. "He's got to go to the hospital. We can't take the responsibility."

When Ernie heard what she intended he locked the door of the laundry. It was his last flare of independence. Right to the end no woman was going to manage him. Lois walked down to the rutile works to ring the ambulance while the desperate Bert broke Ernie's window and got in to him that way. He had had a haemorrhage and was lying in his blood on the floor.

"Don't let her come," Ernie said, as they moved him to the ambulance, and to Lois, "I don't want you."

"I'm coming anyway," Lois told her old adversary, stepping in to tend him on the last journey.

Bert, who drove the car behind the ambulance, broke down and cried. He had loved Ernie all his life. From Port Macquarie Lois sent me a telegram to say that Ernie was in hospital and I was ready packed to leave when the news came next day that Ernie was dead.

They found he had left instructions to be cremated and they had to drive a hundred and fifty miles so that he could have his way. The Returned Soldiers' Association gave him his funeral with a flag draped over the coffin. Lois, taking no notice of Ernie, sent flowers. We sent nothing. We had left him, not for the first time, to wait our coming in vain.

We could not believe we would never see him again, that we had missed him by a week. Everything would be different now and we could hardly bear to come in the gate. "The lake is filling up again," we said as we passed it.

Bert was digging in his garden, Lois in her house getting ready to go to bowls. We went into the clearing over the crossing Ernie had made, through the fence he had put up, working by himself.

The camp oven Ernie had promised to leave me in his will stood by the fire. Ernie's pick and shovel were in a dry place under the tank stand. We tried to feel our loss. Bert was demolishing Ernie's hut over by the bee-yard. Someone had robbed the bees, leaving a scattering of old comb and some wax in a tin tub.

But when we tried to remember Ernie had died there

was no absence of Ernie. It was as though he was just coming into the clearing. He would always be standing, just out of range of your eyes in the shadows of the paperbarks, silent-footed, bare-headed, his beard, his old grey flannel undershirt tucked into the harness strap that held up the greenish corduroys. He had simply not gone away. He had not gone anywhere at all. He was still there and we, as usual, came back, went away, and returned again.

A year later, my son coming back from Dimandead, said, "You were right about Ernie. He's still there." Somehow the memory of his old army hat has left him. He is always bareheaded in the sunlight. If I did not turn round Ernie could be heard talking of the weather and the birds. Dimandead shines now with more splendid light. It is not every day that a headland takes to itself the soul of a man.

At first we thought that Ernie might have been waiting for us, but Jack took another view. "He was always that obstinate," he said. "Told me he'd die when he was good and ready in his own time. Nobody was going to tell him how to live and how to die either. If he wanted to do a thing he would, and if he didn't he wouldn't. Always suited himself and his own convenience. Apart from that, he's lazy. Loiters around just looking at this and that. 'People have got one way of doing things,' he says. 'I've got another.' And be-the-Gawd, nobody would stop him from having his own way."